DRAGON SHIELD 2

THE LONDON PRIDE

Typeset in Garamond by Avon DataSet Ltd,
Bidford-on-Avon, Warwickshire

Printed and bound in Great Britain by Clays Ltd, St Ives plc

The paper and board used in this paperback by Hodder Children's Books
are natural recyclable products made from wood grown in sustainable
forests. The manufacturing processes conform to the environmental
regulations of the country of origin.

Hodder Children's Books
a division of Hachette Children's Books
338 Euston Road, London NW1 3BH
An Hachette UK company

www.hachette.co.uk

DRAGON SHIELD 2

THE LONDON PRIDE

CHARLIE FLETCHER

Illustrated by Nick Tankard

Hodder
Children's
Books

A division of Hachette Children's Books

For Joe and Alfie Ions, heroes in training

The story so far . . .

In the British Museum, Bast, an ancient Egyptian goddess, has been accidentally freed from thousands of years of frozen captivity. In revenge, she has cast a spell, freezing all the normal people in London.

Only a brother and sister, Will and Jo, have escaped her magic.

The statues of London are alive and moving, divided into human ones (Spits), and non-human ones like animals, gargoyles and especially dragons (Taints). Some Spits have helped Jo and Will, and have just paid the price by being frozen like the people of London.

Bast has sent the dragons after Will and Jo . . .

1

Running scared

Two children were running away from the British Museum as fast as possible, which was not as fast as either would have liked, because of Jo's old injury. She hobble-ran as fast as she could, but her brother Will could see that her leg hurt badly. He kept his eye out for a bicycle or a shopping trolley they could use as a wheelchair, but though the dark streets were full of unmoving people, all he had found so far were a rack of city-bikes for hire, solidly locked in place, and useless to them.

He was trying not to think how horrible it was to be the only mobile things in the eerie, magical freeze-frame that the city had become. The empty sensation in the pit of his stomach made him feel like if he let go he might just fall into himself and disappear. This shaky connection with reality wasn't helped by the fact that they were running in company with Little Tragedy – a small bronze boy – and a large marble dog, Filax.

Jo stumbled to a stop and hung onto a railing outside a house in the middle of a long terrace of Georgian buildings running down one side of the street. She had a stitch, and her leg was hurting badly.

'Just give me a minute,' she said.

They looked up and down the road. Brick and stucco houses stretched away on one side. On the other, a white stone Art Deco building loomed over them. LONDON SCHOOL OF HYGIENE AND TROPICAL MEDICINE was carved above the door. Although the streetlamps were not lit, there was a light on in a building opposite, and the strange golden ornaments on the black ironwork outside the windows caught it and glinted down at them: snakes, rats, massive mosquitoes and huge bugs that looked like giant ticks and were the size of hubcaps.

'That's creepy,' panted Jo. Biology was one of her favourite subjects at school. She wanted to be a vet. 'A giant bedbug.'

'No dragons though,' said Will. 'You OK?'

'Yeah,' she lied. 'I don't mind running . . . but do we know where we're running to?'

Will shrugged. He didn't. And that was the problem. He knew they had to do something, that they needed a plan. He just didn't know what it was.

'Will,' said Jo. 'We're just thrashing, aren't we?'

He knew what she meant. 'Thrashing' was what you did when you were losing in a video game as the level got too hard, and you just began flailing around wildly. Thrashing was almost always what happened just before you got killed. But this wasn't a video game. There was no automatic 'saved game' to reboot to. This was real.

He reached over and squeezed her hand. At first she looked surprised. Then she squeezed it back.

'Leg's bad, isn't it?' he said.

'Like someone's hitting it with a hammer,' she admitted.

She almost never talked about her pain. So when she did, Will knew it was serious. He needed to get her somewhere to rest. But the moment of contact with her skin, which was warm, reminded him of the frozen people. They were not only frozen in the sense of not moving, they were beginning to get cold.

Initially, when they had tried to move their mother, she had been immobile but warm. Now the people around them were chilled. And knowing his mother was out there, unmoving and cold as stone, froze something inside him too. This wasn't the time to

5

thrash. This was the time to get their heads straight.

He was about to say this when Filax braced himself and growled a warning, the shaggy fur on his shoulders bristling into a ruff as he did so.

2

Bast the Mighty

Bast the Mighty, Bast the Huntress, Bast the so-nearly-Omnipotent that she had frozen almost an entire city, making its citizens look like mere statues, had a nasty feeling that she was, at this precise moment, also dangerously close to being Bast the Ridiculous.

She shouldn't feel like this. She had taken swift revenge on the city's soldier-statues when they had tried to assault her stronghold in the British Museum in an attempt to break her spell. The military statues had helped Will, the only unfrozen boy in London, to rescue Jo, who had been – until Bast stopped her moving – the only unfrozen girl. They'd been shielded from Bast's magic because they wore matching friendship bracelets with beads carved like scarab beetles on them – which just happened to be ancient protective amulets. Bast's curse had detonated a blast-wave of pure blue light, radiating out from the museum and paralysing and punishing every uniformed statue in the city, so they were now as unmoving as the people. The force of her magic was terrifyingly strong.

And yet there she was; Bast – mightiest Bast, Lion Goddess, Protector of Pharaohs, Defender of the Sun God, The Lady of Flame and Eye of Ra – shivering on top of a forty-foot pole, skinny and weak, looking just like any old house cat stuck up a tree in someone's back garden.

Except it wasn't a tree, it was a totem pole. And it wasn't in a back garden, it was in the Central Courtyard of the British Museum. Yet it was a humiliating position for any self-respecting feline, let alone an ancient goddess wakened after millennia of imprisonment inside the bronze form of an ear- and nose-ringed cat.

She was not shivering with fear. She had won the battle. But doing so cost her. The setting of a curse drained what strength she had and made her groggy. Magic uses muscles too, hidden and secret muscles of the mind. It was like going for a run after a long time of taking no exercise at all. She ached. Her head hurt. She coughed as if she was trying to clear an immovable furball. She had the heart of a lioness, the most feared of all the hunters in Africa, deadlier by far than the male. And yet all she wanted to do was

8

put aside her anger, curl up and sleep.

And that made Bast the Mighty mighty angry.

HURRY UP AND GET ME DOWN FROM HERE, she growled.

Two black basalt statues of lion-women were climbing up the totem pole, gingerly using the noses, beaks and grimacing mouths of the carved faces as fingerholds as they pulled themselves towards her.

It was humiliating. One of her claws was stuck fast in the dense old wood, driven deep in like a nail. The lion-women would have to pull it out and free her. She would have revenge for this.

No one embarrasses a god.

Not without suffering the most horrible revenge.

Not without suffering it for a very long time. And not without it being the kind of revenge that is spoken of in terror for generations after it is over.

Bast the Humiliated watched her servants haul their human bodies up the redwood pole and noted how they kept their lion heads tilted away from her, unwilling to look at her current state, in case they should themselves be punished simply for having witnessed it.

Their fear gave her a small flicker of strength and satisfaction.

HURRY UP, she said. I MUST REGATHER MY STRENGTH. I HAVE A NEW WORLD TO CONQUER. AND TO REMOVE AL OBSTACLES TO MY SUCCESS, THERE IS A BOY AND A GIRL WHO MUST FIRST BE ERASED FROM IT!

3

To the rescue

Jo, Will and Little Tragedy peered nervously down the
street at whatever had got Filax's attention. It was
empty of cars, though there was a bus stuck halfway
round a turn, angling into a side junction and blocking
their view of whatever was beyond it. Will was about
to wonder out loud what the dog was growling at,
when Filax barked, two deep warning sounds that
rumbled out of his deep chest and seemed to shake the
ground beneath their feet. Then they heard a wailing
noise like a broken siren and saw fragments of
movement through the side windows of the bus:
something – or things – were coming up the street
behind it at speed, but before they could move or even
think of hiding they saw it was three dark men running
towards them, and right behind was something
altogether bigger and more thunderous.

The men were wearing steel helmets, and for a
happy fragment of a second Will thought that the

11

soldier-statues must have been freed from the cat's curse and were moving again, but as the black metal figures came close he recognised them as firemen from the memorial at St Paul's, the ones who had used their hoses to make the Ghost Church out of nothing but water and light and the memory of the absent building that had been bombed to nothingness in the Great Blitz. But before he could process that disappointment his attention was taken by the great thundering contraption that appeared to be chasing them.

Four galloping bronze horses careered round the back of the bus, pulling a huge high-sided chariot. One of the two wheels came off the ground as it made the corner, and then smacked back onto the tarmac with a mighty crash.

As it hurtled towards them it became clear that the wailing noise was not some kind of faulty warning siren but the yells of a bare-chested bronze boy who was holding the reins and thus – in theory – driving the thing. From the fact that he seemed to be shouting a frenzied, non-stop 'Whoa!' without any visible slowing of the charging horses, it was clear that events had run away with him; the horses were in charge and he was just in the chariot as a kind of noisy hood-ornament.

However, when the firemen skidded to a stop in front of them, the horses did follow suit, so that the whole running bunch suddenly stacked up nose-to-nose with Filax, who – Will noticed – didn't budge an inch.

'That dog there safe?' asked the lead fireman.

'Safe as pie,' said Tragedy with a relieved grin, though he didn't say why pie should be particularly safe. 'Wotcher, Quad!'

He waved at the boy with the reins, who was dragging himself back into the chariot, having been thrown nearly clean out of his precarious cockpit by the sudden halt of his horses. He grinned and waved back, a smile much like Tragedy's cracking his face.

'Hello, Tradge!' he said. 'Strange days, ain't they?'

'They is indeed,' said Tragedy. 'This here is Will and this is Jo, and they're my new mates.'

He pointed at the grinning charioteer. 'And this is Quad,' he said. 'One of my old mates.'

'Quad?' said Jo.

'Short for Quadriga Boy,' said Tragedy. 'The Quadriga is the name of his infernal chariot—'

'And it *is* an infernal chariot,' agreed the boy. 'On account of the horses being so wilful and ungovernable, like.'

'What's going on?' said Tragedy.

'The soldiers have all been frozen,' said the fireman. Will noticed that while he spoke, the other firemen stayed vigilant, their eyes scanning the night sky as if expecting something dangerous to drop out of it at any moment. Their air of alertness was a bit unnerving.

'We know that,' said Will. 'That's why we're running away.'

The fireman grunted. It wasn't a grunt that contained much approval either.

'You can run all you like. Lucky you. But they can't run. They can't move a bleeding inch, can they? And if they're not back on their plinths by midnight they will never move again,' he said, looking at Tragedy. 'You know how it works.'

'Cor!' said Tragedy. 'Cor, you're right. I wasn't thinking.'

'Well, come on then!' said the fireman. 'All hands to the pump. We've got to drag them back to their plinths ourselves. Because if we don't, they're going to be dead forever!'

'He's right,' said Tragedy, looking at Jo and Will. 'I wasn't thinking straight. I was too scared. I'd better be off to lend a hand.'

'You're not big enough to carry a statue,' said Will.

He didn't want to lose their one guide in this strange city they had got trapped in.

'No. I've got to do this,' said Tragedy. 'I mean, I bet I could carry one of them little St Georges if I had to . . .'

The memory of the cheerful and brave Georges who had ridden to their rescue stung Will. He had not only been grateful to them, he had liked them. They had been funny and irreverent and had stuck up for him when the snootier soldier-statues had not taken him seriously. He wanted to help too.

He looked at Jo. She nodded.

'You stay,' said Tragedy. He pointed at the dog. 'Filax here'll be a good guard dog for you.'

'No,' insisted Will. 'We're coming with you.'

He watched Jo limp across to the chariot.

'The soldiers got frozen because they came to help us,' he said. 'We can rest when we've repaid the favour.'

He helped her up and into the chariot.

'This is better than thrashing,' he said.

'And much easier on my knee than all that running,' Jo replied. 'I can ride on this and we can keep an eye on the sky and watch out for dragons.'

She looked a question at the firemen.

The shape of their tin hats reminded Will of the Fusilier who had saved him. In the kind of clear moment you sometimes get when you're very tired, he realised he had liked him because he reminded him of their father, who was also a soldier. He felt a pang of guilt, and then a sudden boost of energy as he realised what they should do next. It was the tiniest first seed of a plan, and though small, it was the end of thrashing around in panic.

'That is what you're watching the sky for, isn't it?' said Jo to the nearest fireman.

'Yes,' he said. 'Dragons and worse.'

Will joined Tragedy and his sister, stowing the dragon shield on the floor, keeping it in place with his foot and holding onto the insides of the chariot as the firemen climbed onto the outside and hung on there. It lurched into motion as Quad snapped the reins and the four horses snorted and leapt forwards.

He looked at Jo. She smiled grimly at him.

'Dragons and worse?' she said. He looked back at her. She was scanning the strip of sky above them. 'What could be worse than dragons?'

Not for the first time Will thought she was much braver than he was.

'Don't know,' he said, trying to sound normal.

And older. And more intrepid. And cool. 'Wish we didn't have to find out. But I expect we will . . .'

As they raced away, they left the street behind them to the eerie and unmoving silence that had bewitched everything – or almost everything. And because they were scanning the sky and the way ahead they didn't spare a look backwards. So they missed the two golden rats on the School of Hygiene and Tropical Medicine, who shifted slightly, their noses wrinkling and tails lashing as they smelled the air. Nor did they see one of the giant, bird-sized mosquitoes detaching from the ironwork and hanging in the air beneath its humming wings, like a drone.

Jo looked at Will.

'Why are you smiling?' she said.

'Because we needed a plan,' he said. 'And if the statues are healed at midnight, then maybe they'll be healed from being frozen too. And then we can talk to the Fusilier.'

'Who?' she said.

'You didn't meet him. He saved me after you got taken by the dragons. But he's the one I trust,' he said. 'You'll like him. He feels . . . safe, you know? He's a bit like Dad. He got melted saving me. I reckon he's the one that'll have the best plan.'

'OK,' she agreed. 'Maybe he can tell us how to help Mum too.'

'Fusilier's a good egg,' said Tragedy, who'd been listening. 'Talking to him's a good plan.'

'Maybe he can help us to help everyone,' said Will.

Behind them, unseen, the mosquito tipped in the air and drifted slowly after them.

4

Four dragons

A dead dragon should at the very least be majestic. The merest glimpse of its corpse should chill the bones of any viewer and inspire a bowel-loosening sense of dread at the horrific fact that even the most magnificent and fabulous of creatures can perish. It should be awe-inspiring.

The very sight of slain dragon should change the world.

The lifeless thing impaled on the railings round Coram's Fields was not majestic. Not any more. He was sad. He wasn't fabulous either, or awe-inspiring. He was awkward and – frankly – ridiculous. He had expired in a particularly ungainly and self-destructive fashion when Will had used his own shield to ricochet the twisting spirals of his fire-jet back onto him. This had heated the dragon to the point where he first became welded to the iron railings and then collapsed in an undignified slump, the spikes on top of the railing sliding through him like hot skewers through a pat of butter.

As he had cooled, so he had become part of the railings themselves, a twisted, half-melted flail of wings and talons. His legs, claws, tail and horribly skewed neck all pointed in different directions, turning him into a grotesque, silvered bomb-burst, frozen into a permanent 3D splat and pinned in place by the line of black spikes that passed straight through him.

And, worse than not being majestic, he was clearly a problem.

Two identical dragons, unmelted, mobile and entirely normal (as much as a fire-breathing flying lizard the size of a skip can be normal) stood in front of him with cocked heads and deeply furrowed brows. They'd laid their shields on the pavement beside them, and had the distinct air of workmen about to execute a necessary but rather unwelcome task.

One of them stepped up to the dead dragon and tugged him by the wingtip.

He didn't move. The other shouldered past with a huff of frustration and took a businesslike two-taloned grip of the impaled dragon's torso. His muscular thighs flexed and bunched as he tried to slide the body off the railings.

He didn't move at all.

The first dragon gave a huff of his own, which had a distinct 'told you so' edge to it.

Next they both tried to lift together.

The dragon didn't budge an inch off the railings, but the railings themselves started to work free of the crumbling concrete in which they were embedded. The horizontal bars that held them in place began to bow upwards with the force the two dragons were exerting, but after a moment they gave up, and the railings whanged back into place with a loud concussion of metal on stone.

The dragons looked at each other.

One looked back at the transfixed dragon and cocked his head sideways, allowing his stubby arms to reach the top of his head and give it a puzzled scratch.

He made a noise that sounded distinctly like 'Ook?'

The other one looked over his head, into the sky, and made an answering noise that was definitely an 'Ulp . . .' And it wasn't any old 'Ulp'. It was the kind of 'Ulp . . .' that clearly meant 'Uh-oh . . .' in any language.

The head-scratcher followed his eyeline and saw the incoming shape gliding out of the sky.

He stepped back and stood waiting with the other

one. Both of them dropped their heads and folded their ears back, like guilty dogs about to be scolded for doing something unmentionable.

The incoming third dragon snapped back his wings with a tremendous thunder-crack, and then beat downwards with such perfect timing that he killed his inbound velocity and landed with a delicacy that made him appear to have just stepped out of the air. He was, in fact, a whole different class of dragon to the silver ones busy trying not to cower in front of him like a pair of naughty schoolboys. They, like all the city dragons, looked rather stocky and mass-produced. This wasn't their fault. It was how they had been ordered by the city fathers who had commissioned them. They were workmanlike and very effectively dragonish. Nine times out of ten the impression they created on the viewer was entirely satisfactory: they emanated a stolid aura and were – due to the bright-red and silver paint job – real eye-catchers. It was only when seen next to the other dragon (who was known as the Temple Bar dragon from the spot he normally occupied outside the The Royal Courts of Justice on the Strand) that people realised how much they lacked. The Temple Bar dragon was not stocky, painted nor mass-produced: he was the work of a far more talented artist than the municipal sculptor; he was wiry and spiky and savage and distinctly dangerous. He oozed peril. His face was haughty and commanding, his deep-set eyes terrifying and fiercely intelligent. He had the air of a steel mainspring flexed to near-breaking point, and the pent-up energy he exuded made him look like the worst trouble just about to happen: a cocked gun on a hair-trigger, a nightmare on the point of coming true in the most lethal fashion.

He was the master of all the other dragons, brighter, sharper and more deadly. If they had been made to guard the city, he was the leader of the guard, and he was the reason the other two dragons were now looking both very shamefaced and anywhere but directly into his cold, unforgiving eyes.

He stared at them until they found their gaze rising to meet his against their better judgement, forced to do so by the power of his will.

'Ulp,' said one, in answer to the unspoken question.

'Ook,' his companion added quietly.

The Temple Bar dragon stepped across the pavement and looked at the disastrously impaled corpse. He exhaled slowly, like a very patient but still irritated steam-boiler. He rapped the knuckles of his fore-claws against the breastbone of the unmoving creature. He poked at the railings skewering it in place. Then he shook his head and looked at the two dragons with eyes that mixed disappointment with equal parts of pity and frustration.

Then he took a long breath inwards, unnaturally long, inhaling so deeply that the air howled as it was sucked down the long stretch of his thin, muscular neck. He clamped his pointy jaws shut and let the hotness build in the fire-crop at the base of his throat, until his breastbone glowed red with the banked-up heat, and then he aimed his mouth at the base of the railings just below the messily spatchcocked dragon and breathed out.

The multicoloured blast of wildfire that shot from within him was a jet braided from blue and yellow and orange and purple and red flames. He played it back and forth across the iron paling, carefully avoiding the dragon's body, but getting as close to it as he could. As he washed the fiery stream over the railings, they themselves began to change colour as they heated up – going from black to grey, then to orange, red then pink and then, as the railings reached white heat, he snapped his talons at the other two dragons.

They leapt forwards and gripped the fallen dragon,

sliding it cleanly off the spikes.

As soon as it was clear, the Temple Bar dragon choked off the stream of wildfire and turned to look at the corpse, which the others had laid carefully on the ground.

He bent and touched the smoking holes left by the railings, and shook his head in disapproval. He emitted a chuff of angry wildfire that bowled through the park fence and accidentally ignited the contents of a nearby rubbish bin. This made him even more irritated. He gestured to the other dragons, one of whom hopped the railings, stood over the bin and blew the fire out with one thunderous blast of air.

They were, after all, city dragons, and no matter what the cat had got them doing, they were instinctively protective of the fabric of the place. Setting fire to London was the last thing they'd want to be caught doing, even by accident.

By the time he hopped back over the railings, the Temple Bar dragon had stood straight and got his anger under control. He nodded to the others, who picked up their shields with one claw, and then each took hold of an arm of the fallen dragon with the other, clearly about to carry him away with them.

The Temple Bar dragon coughed. His raised

eyebrow and the talon he was pointing at their shields made the question clear: where was the shield of the fallen dragon?

Clearly the 'Ulp' and 'Ook' he got in response was not satisfactory. He chuffed in irritation again. Then he waved them off. They stumbled their way into the sky looking distinctly and comically like two ungainly drinkers escorting a third, and much drunker, friend homewards. They headed south.

The Temple Bar dragon didn't look a bit comical. He looked deadly serious. He cracked his wings open and hurled himself at the night, heading west, towards the unnatural glow now surrounding the distant British Museum like a ghostly blue dome.

5

Dunkirk by chariot

Running away was one thing, but running back was quite another kettle of fish. In fact, it was probably a pretty old and unrefrigerated kettleful, because it stank, especially when you were running back into the danger you'd begun by running away from in the first place.

As the chariot bumped and swerved through the streets, Will caught Jo's eye. She nodded, as if able to read his thoughts.

'I'm trying to remember what Dad always says about being brave,' she said. 'That it's not about doing something fearlessly, but being scared, and then doing it anyway. You know?'

He nodded. His mouth was too dry to reply.

She grimaced. 'It sounded good when he said it. But it's not really helping me much.'

'I know,' he grunted. It wasn't helping him much either. Nor was seeing how white and drawn his sister's face was.

He looked down and found he was unconsciously rotating the scarab on the bracelet round his wrist. He stopped, suddenly aware the string was fraying a bit. He didn't want to lose its protection. He should have it on something solid, like the metal loop his mother kept hers on, attached to her . . .

'. . . Key ring!' he said.

'What?' said Jo.

'Mum's got another scarab on her key ring, hasn't she?' he said excitedly. 'We could put it round her wrist and then she'd be able to move like us!'

Jo sat up. 'Brilliant.' Then she sank back and looked at the passing streetscape, visibly hit by immediate second thoughts.

'But, Will, imagine her waking up in all this. I mean, we sort of eased into it as it first happened. It might shock her too much . . .'

'You mean send her loopy?' he said.

'Or give her a heart attack or something,' she said. 'It is sort of like a vision of hell, or your worst ever nightmare isn't it?'

'We'd be there,' he said uncertainly. 'I mean, we could help her get her head round it . . .' He didn't sound convincing, even to himself.

'So you're saying we should go there now?' she said,

29

sounding equally tentative. 'Yeah. Maybe you're right.'

It's not always great when people agree with you. Especially when their voices are betraying the same doubt you're feeling. He tried to think straight.

'Well, I don't think we should be going anywhere by ourselves,' he said, backtracking a bit. 'I don't think that's sensible or safe. And I think if we have the chance of going to help Mum, we should go with the Fusilier because he has a gun and can stand up to dragons, and we can't.'

'OK,' she said. 'OK. That's sensible. That's a good plan too.'

'Running off to Mum now, not knowing what was watching us in the dark would be thrashing,' he said. 'It'd be . . . foolhardy.'

Never in his life had he used the word 'foolhardy' before. He must really be reaching for excuses, he thought, caught between the tug towards his mother and the knowledge that if her extra scarab was indeed their one big chance, it was important to make sure they got it safely, rather than lose it by snatching hurriedly at it.

And even as he thought this, a weasel voice at the back of his head sneered at him and told him he was making excuses for his cowardice.

'I'm just saying that if there's a chance of doing it with an armed escort . . .'

'Will,' Jo said, half laughing. 'I get it! Armed escort? Good idea. You're barging through an open door! It's what Dad would say, right? The 7Ps.'

Their dad always went on about the 7Ps, which was an army training thing to remind you why charging ahead without a plan was a really bad idea. In fact, Will had also realised that the 7Ps were a good thing to remember when gaming, to avoid thrashing. So Jo bringing them up now was spot on the money and made him feel good again.

'Proper Prior Planning Prevents Pathetically Poor Performance,' he grinned, reciting the 7Ps like a comforting spell. 'Maybe the Fusilier will—'

The thing dropped straight out of the night sky above them without warning, filling the road with its wings, stopping them like a roadblock.

It happened so fast that they were all thrown forwards into the front of the chariot, and by the time they had untangled themselves enough to peer over the edge, Will had convinced himself that a large black dragon was waiting to roast them and then tear them to bits.

It wasn't a dragon. It was another winged woman,

with a stern face and flowing robes and the wingspan of a light aircraft. She was already talking earnestly to the three firemen who were standing in front of her looking up into her eyes.

One of the strangest things about her was that she had another winged figure held under her arm, like a piece of luggage. With a nasty shock Will recognised the flying helmet of the pilot who had crashed to earth when the Mighty Bast had cursed all the military statues into immobility. He could still hear the terrible metallic crashing KER-DOING the pilot had made as he hit the courtyard flagstones.

'Right,' she was saying in a clipped and commanding voice like a severe schoolteacher addressing a rather slow group of students. 'We're clearing all the casualties out of the museum front yard first, and then working our way back from there. We don't know what's going on in the museum but that's where the danger's centred. You three cut along there now and see what you can carry.'

'That's my Victory,' said Quad, turning to Jo and Will. 'She's normally on top of us on the arch.'

Will could remember how the statue on top of the Wellington Arch normally looked, with the winged angel at the highest point so that it almost looked like she was driving the chariot. Most people didn't notice the yelling Quad holding the reins beneath her.

'She's got huge wings,' said Jo.

'I know,' said Quad approvingly. 'Keep the rain off me, they do.'

'I am not your umbrella, young Quad,' said the Victory, her eyes snapping up and catching Jo and Will. 'Ah. I had heard there were two regular people still moving. I hadn't expected them to be so . . . small.'

'Small?' said Jo, with just the hint of an edge to her voice.

Will put a hand on her shoulder. This didn't seem a good time to be making an enemy of a thirty-foot angel.

'We're here to help,' said Jo.

The Victory raised an eyebrow and cocked her head on one side.

'The soldiers helped us,' said Will.

'We thought we could handle the little St Georges,' chimed in Tragedy. 'Free up some of you bigger ones to deal with the larger soldiers. And they want to see the Fusilier who's down near the St George's plinths, see? See if they can talk to him after midnight heals all.'

As he heard Tragedy explaining, Will felt as though his plan was quite well-joined up. His heart lifted a bit.

The Victory uncocked her head and lowered the eyebrow.

'Good idea,' she said. 'Though we do not yet know if midnight will heal the broken *and* remove the spell too. We've never seen magic like this.'

Will's cheerfulness lurched downwards again.

'Now, stay back here and wait,' said the Victory. 'We'll bring them to you. No idea what's in the museum or when it might come out fighting.'

'It's a cat,' said Jo. 'A cat with earrings. Egyptian. And it has lion-headed women as its soldiers.'

'Does it indeed,' said the Victory. She nodded to herself. 'Egyptian cat, eh? Interesting.'

'See?' said Tragedy. 'They've already been useful.'

'They have,' said the Victory. 'Thank you. We shall ponder it. Now, wait back here and we'll bring you the Georges. We've a lot of soldiers to move before midnight or it will be disastrous. It's going to be Dunkirk all over again, except by land.'

She rose, wings swirling the air into a down draught that buffeted them as she turned and flapped towards the museum.

'Dunkirk?' said Tragedy. 'Who's he?'

'It's not a he,' said Jo.

'She, then,' said Tragedy. 'Pardon me. I ain't

34

educated like some.'

'It's a place,' said Will, remembering his history lessons. 'In the Second World War the army got stuck on the wrong side of the English Channel and all the little boats and ships of Britain went over and brought them home, all higgledy-piggledy, little yachts and pleasure-steamers and coal barges and whatever floated. Ordinary people did it, saving the soldiers. Because they couldn't save themselves.'

Tragedy looked round.

'Well, we're ordinary enough,' he said. 'We better get on with it.'

There was a pause.

'I should like to take a peek round the corner though.' Tragedy stepped off the chariot. 'You coming?'

'Will?' said Jo.

'I'll be right back,' he replied. 'It's just up there; I'm not going far.'

He followed Tragedy the fifty metres to the corner and looked around. There were figures moving everywhere, stone and bronze statues of all ages and sizes weaving through the forest of frozen humanity, gingerly carrying the unmoving bodies of military statues as they wound their way through the maze.

Will had felt torn about coming to see this, worried

about leaving even fifty metres between him and Jo, but when he saw the crowd of helpers working together to rescue the fallen, he knew he'd done the right thing. Of all the weirdness he had witnessed since time stopped and the dragons began moving, this was the most strange, and he would not, he admitted to himself, have missed seeing it for anything.

He was watching two worlds impossibly coming together, not colliding, but passing through each other. The statues took care not to knock any of the people, but only in the way you wouldn't want to walk into a tree trunk if you were walking through a forest, and the people . . . Well, as far as he knew, they could not see any of this, and if they did, they would not remember it when they started moving again. *If* they started moving again.

He saw strange combinations as they passed – bewigged politicians and aristocrats carrying tin-hatted soldiers from both world wars on their shoulders as if they were carrying a boat between them. He saw winged Victories and angels labouring in flight just below the level of the rooftops as they carried away stiff bronze bodies hanging from each hand. He saw a statue he recognised as the Officer from the Artillery Memorial, the one who had led the sortie against the museum, being trundled past on another chariot, this one driven by two fierce girls in flowing robes.

'Oi!' said Tragedy. 'Icy Girls, where's your mum then?'

One of the girls looked at him.

'She stopped moving like these ones. We left her behind.'

As they passed, Tragedy turned to Will.

'Their mum. Boudicca, Queen of the Iceni. Call her the Red Queen, we do, cos she was such a warrior. S'pose that's why she's stopped too.'

The firemen ran up. They were carrying two small statues and a big one of a soldier in a tall bearskin hat with a long bayonet on the end of his musket.

'Come on,' they said. 'No time for standing round gawking with your mouths open. Thought you wanted to help!'

They put the big statue into the back of Quad's chariot and wedged the two smaller ones on either side of it. They were indeed the St Georges who had made friends with Will, and he had seen that they made up for their size with speed and bravery: they wore armour but had their heads bare, heads that looked much too modern for their medieval get-up, like a couple of 'jolly good chaps' from the 1920s. Which is, in one way, exactly what he had found them to be: jolly good and willing to sacrifice themselves to help rescue his sister.

There was something else about them that had changed.

'They're glowing a bit,' he said. 'Bluish . . .'

The fireman closest to him nodded.

'They all are. Something to do with whatever is stopping them moving.'

Will remembered the blue light from within the museum, and the chanting and the blue flash that had radiated out from it as Bast had roared her curse. He looked more closely at the statues. There was a thin coating on them, not quite like a frost, more like a skin of water that wasn't wet and didn't slide off the metal beneath.

'No time to hang around,' said the fireman. 'You get these two back to Grays Inn Road. Then, Quad, you go like the clappers and get this Grenadier back to Pall Mall. You'll be cutting it fine, so get a ruddy bend on.'

Will and Jo held on tight as Quad flicked the reins and set them in motion, overtaking a pair of marble women in togas who were carrying a heavily bemedalled soldier in Victorian dress uniform sporting an impressively lavish moustache and a surprised expression on his unmoving face.

'Mind your backs, ladies!' whooped Tragedy. And they were off.

And as they jinked through the stalled traffic and the groups of statues rescuing other statues, the worst thing was not the unfamiliarity of it all, or the slight seasicky feeling caused by the swervy stop–start motion. It was that the streets – frozen in time before the lights had come on – were not as dark as they had been.

'It's the people as well,' said Jo. 'They're getting a blue glow too.'

She was right. The thin film, the not-quite-frost and not-quite-wetness that coated the statues was also covering the people, making them glow a faint blue that – when the pavements were crowded – provided their own source of light.

What neither of them said, as they passed these knots of people, glowing in the dark, was that somewhere in the city their mother was like this, encased in a skein of blue magic, unmoving and alone.

The thought of this kept them quiet for a good ten minutes. Will saw they were on High Holborn and picking up speed as they got closer and closer to the Fusiliers Monument in the middle of the street. He saw the broken-backed figure in the distance and felt like retching at the sight of it.

'It's getting worse,' said Will. 'I think it's my fault.'

'Will,' said Jo. 'Why does everything have to be your fault! It's like you're totally addicted to being guilty or something. It's not healthy. And this whole thing isn't our fault. Everything freezing is not your fault.'

'Not the city freezing, that's not my fault,' he agreed. 'But the soldiers? Think that's down to me. Was my fault you got taken by the dragon, so it's my fault they had to rescue you. And because they helped me, this happened. Because of me, it got much, much worse.'

She looked at him.

'You're SUCH a misery guts,' she said. 'And you know how they say misery loves company?'

He nodded.

'Well, sometimes company doesn't love misery back, Will! Sometimes company thinks misery is a real pain in the—'

The chariot came to a sudden halt and they had to grab on to avoid being thrown forwards.

'Look out!' said Tragedy, pointing at two winged shapes dropping out of the sky in front of them. 'Here comes trouble . . .'

6

Bathed in blue

Bast the Mighty had allowed her lion-headed hand-maidens to carry her back into the Egyptian Sculpture Gallery. The museum curators were still frozen in the fatefully unwise act of replacing the broken chunk in the black sarcophagus. It had been unwise because in doing so they'd completed the strip of picture-writing ringing the sarcophagus. Blue light had immediately swept round it, activating a charm freeing Bast from the curse that had penned her immobile inside the body of a small bronze cat, and allowing her to freeze them and the rest of the city in an instant. And although for the moment she remained stuck within the cat-shaped prison, she could now at least move around in it, controlling the body of the cat as if it were her own.

The sarcophagus was now brimful of the blue light so that it looked like a black bathtub full of fluorescent water. But the pool of blue light was not there to clean; it was there to revive. It was the source of all the power that had changed the city according to Bast's wishes, and when she had exhausted herself with her exertions, all she needed to do was to get back in the tub and let the power recharge her.

However, she was too shaken and dishevelled to climb into the deep bath-shaped depression under her own steam, and allowed the lioness-women to gently lower her into the blue light. She curled up beneath the surface, nose to tail, and closed her eyes.

Already she could feel the magical energy soaking into her. The gold ear- and nose-rings glowed and vibrated with a thrumming noise, a sound that was suspiciously like the noise an ordinary cat makes when it is happy. It was an unnatural purring though, and at the sound of it the lionesses stepped back and exchanged looks but not words.

The resonance they were feeling quivered and pulsed through the floor and walls of the entire museum, as if it was breathing, as if it was becoming an extension of the Mighty Bast's own body. The lionesses did not step back in fear. They stepped back in respect for a power that had been old long before the birth of the quarrymen who had hacked out the blocks of black stone from which they had been sculpted more than three thousand years ago.

7

Soho Sal

The winged figures that dropped out of the sky were not dragons. Filax, running beside the chariot, stopped but did not growl at them. Instead he wagged his tail.

They were the Angels of Mercy from the war memorial next to the small St George's plinths in the inner courtyard of the cathedral-like Prudential building across the street.

They had stopped the chariot in the middle of High Holborn, conveniently almost next to the ruined statue of the Fusilier. The Fusilier had taken wildfire right in his mouth, swallowing a fire-hose of flame that had entered his body and melted it so badly that his top half now flapped down over his back, like a frozen molten wave. It was a horrible reminder to Will of what he might be responsible for.

Things happened rather quickly. The Angels were worried that there wasn't enough time to get the Georges back and deliver the bearskinned soldier to his plinth before midnight. Quad promised he could do it if he and Tragedy 'travelled light and drove like the clappers'. Jo and Will would wait here until Tragedy returned. It was decided they would be safe enough under the eyes of the Angels, and that, suddenly, was that.

'It's all a bit confused,' said an Angel of Mercy as they watched the chariot career off down the street. 'It's not like there's anyone planning things at all sensibly over there. I mean, I can't think why they had that Grenadier and these Georges in the same load. They're from entirely different ends of town. Are you all right with one George between you?'

She looked at them both and the two frozen knights on the tarmac next to them, where Tragedy had rather unceremoniously dumped them beside Filax, who sat there with his tail thumping happily. The Angel scratched his head and the thumping redoubled.

'Yes,' said Jo.

'No,' said Will. 'No. She shouldn't have to carry anything heavy. She's got a bad leg.'

'Hence the stick,' said the Angel. 'Sorry. I should have spotted that. Don't worry. I'll be right back with help; we have time.'

And she picked up one of the Georges and

strode off towards the red-brick portico of the Prudential building.

'I'm not helpless, Will,' said Jo. 'We could manage.'

'I know,' he said. 'But you don't have to.'

The other Angels came out of the arch and swooped down, lifting the George.

'Midnight heals all,' said one of the Angels. 'Come on, you two. Come under cover with us. It's going to rain.'

'No, thanks,' said Will. 'We want to stay here and talk to the Fusilier after he's healed.'

'It's all right,' said one of the Angels, misunderstanding his reasons. 'All the dead dragons have gone. There's nothing to be frightened of in there any more.'

'What happened to them?' he said.

'Some live ones came and took them,' said the Angel.

He gaped at her in surprise.

'Fair's fair,' she said. 'They've got as much right as anyone to be on their plinths at midnight. Taints they may be through no choice of their own, but there's no one so bad as shouldn't get a second chance, is there?'

Will thought of the yowling hellcat that had

attacked him, and the giant scarab. And the dragons that had ganged up and melted the Fusilier. He didn't say anything. None of it made him instinctively feel like forgiving. Maybe you had to be an angel to think like that.

'We'll just stay here and wait for the Fusilier,' he said. 'If that's OK with you?'

They sat on a bench on the pavement, looking across at the Fusilier.

The Angel stared at them for a beat, then nodded and flapped away.

'Shout if you need help,' she said over her shoulder. 'If you keep still enough you probably won't draw the attention of anything bad.'

Jo didn't feel very reassured by that, somehow. Filax came and sat next to her, leaning companionably against her good leg.

'Oi, get off,' said Jo. 'You great lump.'

Filax just wagged his tail. She stroked his head and didn't push him away.

'Jo . . .' said Will.

'I'm fine,' she said.

Will could hear the thickness in her voice. She hated people showing her sympathy even more than she disliked the aching knee and the tortured muscles she carried around everywhere she went. It wasn't just the muscles in her leg; her back also ached because in order to walk anything like normally she had to overcompensate and hide the limp she was stuck with, the visible sign that she loathed so much.

'You know the nicest thing about a dog?' said Will. 'It's that it's nothing like a cat. That one in the museum's put me off them for life.'

She knew what he meant.

They sat quietly together, which was rare. They usually argued or joked, sometimes both at once. But there were times when they both understood silence was OK without having to voice it, and this was one of those times. Being so comfortable with someone that you don't feel every silence needs filling with pointless spraff is the true test of friendship. So they sat there for a while, listening to the entire city not moving around them.

Will's eyes were becoming gritty with tiredness, but he kept dragging them back to stare at the ruined statue in the middle of the street, willing it to be midnight already, willing it to move again.

And then he closed them for a moment.

At least, it felt like a moment, but he snapped awake with the nasty feeling that he'd missed something.

'You were snoring,' said Jo.

'I wasn't, I didn't . . .' He cleared his throat. It felt dry. 'I was, wasn't I?'

'Like a walrus,' said Jo.

'I didn't mean to fall asleep,' he said.

'Doesn't matter,' she said. 'You weren't out long. Maybe quarter of an hour. It isn't midnight yet.'

He looked down the road. Jo looked in the opposite direction and with the tail of her eye thought she caught something flapping by, far overhead, just for an instant casting a moon-shadow that rippled over the empty street, but then it was gone. She kept her eyes on the sky. It might have gone for now, but the glimpse she thought she'd seen had seemed more dragon-shaped than bird-like.

'Oooh, and this must be the famous Will and Jo Show,' said a husky woman's voice behind them.

They turned.

They had seen more strange things in the last day than they had ever even imagined possible, but the statue floating down through the night air was in its own way the strangest thing so far. And since 'so far' had included dragons and giant scarabs and angels, that meant a whole new level of strange.

She was a winged woman, but not like any they had

yet seen. She did not have bird's wings, like the various angels or the Victories. Instead she had the wings of a giant dragonfly, but a dragonfly whose wings were pierced all over with star-shaped cut-outs. Her hair was long and thick, and hung unbound on either side of a strong face with heavy-lidded eyes and generous, wide lips. The folds of a flimsy dress clung to her prominent curves and looked, much as Ariel's strips of material had been, as if it were kept on as much by the wind as anything else.

None of these things, not even the insectile wings whirring behind her, were what made her especially strange: what gave her that extra-special layer of the exotic were the other stars. She was covered with them, and not only stippled and studded with them on her skin, in her hair and all over her clothing, but also orbited by them. They hovered *around* her body but unattached to it, so that she flew through the air surrounded by a personal constellation of stars that moved with her like a force-field. The little stellar cloud shone a pale golden light that twinkled about her as she looked down at them with a lazy and amused smile.

She did not look like someone who ever hurried. She looked languorous and just a little bit theatrical.

Strange garlands trailed from each hand, reaching to her ankles, made of ribbons and masks and knotted posies of little flowers and – of course – more stars.

'Hi,' said Jo hesitantly. 'And you are . . . ?'

'Soho Sal, to you,' said the woman. 'Or Selene, Queen of the Night, if you want to be all formal, though that sounds a bit up itself, don't it?'

Her voice was surprisingly streetwise. It wasn't high-flown like the angels or the Victories, for example. It was low, almost masculine, and it was warm.

'Little Tradge sent me for you. I've come to take you somewhere safe for the night.'

She looked at them.

'It's all right, kids. I've got a hotel all of my very own, and trust me, the way things are, no one's going to mind you shacking up in a nice safe room. And you'll like it. Top of the line, beds soft as powder puffs, and all in all as comfy and luxy a gaff as you'll find anywhere in town, though I say it myself.' And she winked. 'Grab a hand and I'll have you there before you know it.'

Jo exchanged a look with Will.

'Where is Tragedy? He said he'd be back for us.'

'He's somewhere between here and Pall Mall where he and his little mucker Quad are delivering a burly

51

gent in a bearskin before the clock strikes midnight and everyone turns into a permanent pumpkin,' said Selene with a throaty laugh. 'Which will be any minute now. He'll be along before morning. He knows just where you'll be.'

Will looked up at the tortured flame-splash of metal that had been the Fusilier.

'We want to stay,' he said. He needed to see if what he had been told was true. If it was, maybe he wouldn't feel so guilty. 'We want to see if he gets better at midnight.'

'Why wouldn't he?' said Selene. 'That's the way it's always worked. On your plinth by midnight, all the day's sins forgiven, every naughty boy and girl who has scuffed themselves up in the dark bounces back fresh as a daisy, and no one any the wiser.'

'Good,' said Jo. 'Because then we need to talk to him and get moving.'

'Get moving where, lovey?' said Selene.

Will was about to reply when he heard the distant sound of church bells sounding midnight.

'Ooh la la, here we go,' said Selene. 'Look sharp and see if you can catch it. Most can't.'

'What do you mean?' said Will, eyes locked on the broken statue as the bells rang through the carillon that came before the ominous single strokes that would sound out the hour.

'Well, you know like when people say you see a green flash at the moment the sun goes down?' said Selene. 'I mean, they say it, but no matter how hard you try and see it, it's gone before you can, or you blink and miss it.'

The carillon ended, and there was a ponderous beat of silence. Will and Jo stared. Will's eyes began to sting, but he was not going to blink now until the hour sounded. It was like a staring contest. It seemed like the longest short pause ever. How long could it be? He counted in his head. One elephant. Two elephant, three eleph— blink . . . Damn, he thought . . .

He missed it.

At least, he thought he did. Maybe he caught a blur, or perhaps that was his eyelid's involuntary opening and closing to bring relief to his screaming eyeballs. In the silence the Fusilier had been there with his core burned out and melted, his head flopped horribly back down over his shoulders like a grotesque rucksack on a headless torso. Yet as the resonant 'bong' of midnight rang out over the city, he was whole and unbroken, head on his shoulders, staring down High Holborn, eyes steady and alert, rifle held loosely in one hand, leg cocked up on the stony plinth, ready to move at a moment's notice.

Except he didn't.

He looked mended and ready for action. But he didn't move.

'Wow,' said Jo. 'That's cool.'

'Hi!' said Will, looking up into the Fusilier's face. He waved. 'I'm down here. Me, Will . . .'

The Fusilier didn't look down. Didn't move at all. Will walked up to the plinth and looked closer.

'No,' he said, voice catching in disappointment. 'That's frozen. He's mended but still frozen.'

He looked across at Jo.

'So much for the 7Ps,' he said.

'We just make another plan,' she said. She didn't sound convinced. She was trying to put a brave face on it.

'Yup,' he said. 'I'm open to suggestions.'

She shrugged and looked away.

He felt like he'd been punched in the stomach. He'd been pinning all his hopes on the Fusilier coming back to reassuring life and taking charge. But the soldier was covered in the thin, not-quite-water, not-quite-frost layer of blue, like all the rigid and unmoving people on the streets around them, and was no reassurance at all.

'All the soldiers is going to be frozen then, love,' said Selene. 'Midnight doesn't break this blue magic, I reckon. That's going to be the big problem.'

'I know,' he said. 'I just thought that midnight might heal all. I'm sure someone said that.'

'Well,' said Selene. 'May not have healed all, but it cured something. He isn't all twisted and torn like he was. So now he's no worse than the others, and there's every chance he'll be right as a trivet, soon as this all gets back to normal.'

She sounded bright and breezy, but it was the kind of bright breeziness adults put on to cover up the fact they were running on wishes rather than solid fact.

'And exactly how are things going to get back to normal?' Will said. They were still on their own. And still thrashing.

She chuckled and shrugged. When she raised and lowered her shoulders the cloud of stars moved with her, shrugging too.

'Haven't got a Scooby!' she said. 'I'd be lying if I said I did, but shall I tell you what I do know . . .'

'What?' he said.

'Time for you two to come with me. You're falling asleep on your feet.'

She pirouetted between Will and Jo in a slow twirl of sparkling light that enfolded them both as her hands took theirs. Her grip was warm and firm, and as she pulled them within the aura of her sparkling cloud it felt as if the stars were tickling them gently, in the way bubbles in a champagne glass tickle your nose. It wasn't a bad feeling at all. It was surprisingly gentle and comforting and lifting to their spirits, and yet at the same time quite relaxing.

It was so lifting and relaxing that Will noticed he was smiling, and yawned before he noticed they were actually being lifted physically too, as Selene flew them up into the night sky of the new-minted day.

'Wait . . .' he said.

'I think it's OK,' said Jo. 'It feels OK.'

'And I promise you the beds are going to feel ten times better,' said Selene as she wafted them over the rooftops. 'And then after a good night's sleep you'll feel like things ain't so bad after all. Sleep's a great healer. And I should know. I'm a moon goddess, aren't I.'

'Are you?' said Jo.

Selene chuckled.

'I might be. I don't know, tell the truth, quite what I am. Depends on the day. I'm a bit of a hodge-podge of things, like everyone; bit of a mongrel. Moon goddess, lady of the night, sleep-bringer, dream-weaver, sing-a-bit-dance-a-bit girl, sassy star-juggler and all-round bundle of fabulosity is what I am!'

'Fabulosity,' yawned Will. 'S'not even a proper word . . .'

'Who wants to be proper when improper is so much more fun?' she said proudly. 'Anyway it's so much more than a word, isn't it? It's more like a state of being. Now, hold on, we're nearly there.'

Jo looked down at the strange cityscape passing beneath their feet. Rooftops made dark islands around which the streets below seemed to flow like canals, the watery effect made by the bluish light coming from the crowds of static pedestrians on the pavements.

She could see Filax running along beneath them, looking up to check their progress. She tapped Will on the shoulder and pointed.

'That's some guard dog you got there,' said Selene, following the direction of Jo's finger. 'Never seen one like him before. He's tenacious!'

'Have you seen anything like *any* of this before?' Will said.

'No,' said Selene. 'No. But no fears, my dears! If there's one thing I've learned from a life spent stooging round in Soho, it's that nothing new is bad just because you haven't seen it before. Some of the most shockingly new things turn out lovely when you least expect it.'

'And some don't,' said Will.

'But some do,' insisted Selene. 'Chin up. What I believe is the universe likes to even things out. So just like night balances day, good eventually makes up for badness.'

'That's just optimism,' said Will.

'No,' said Selene. 'That's fabulosity.' She grinned at Jo. 'But optimism's a good start too. We're here.'

And she dipped and flew them down towards the front door of a very smart-looking hotel.

'Now. There'll be a room on the fourth floor, on the corner, just for you. Door's open. You'll have to take the stairs. But I'll be up there guarding you all night.'

She pointed at a plinth on the wall directly over the door.

'You'll be safe as hotels, which is much safer than houses. I'm here to guard you, but don't wander about. Sleep tight. And don't leave the room unless it's me or Tragedy comes for you. OK?'

Will wanted to say nothing was OK, that they should be trying to get all this sorted, but the wave of tiredness engulfing him was too strong.

Jo took his arm.

'You want me to carry your shield thing? You look exhausted.'

He looked at her, leaning on her stick, smiling gamely despite the dark rings under her eyes.

'No,' he said, hefting the dragon shield onto his shoulder by the strap. 'No. I'm fine. But Selene – I mean Sal – is right: we need to sleep.'

There was a panting noise and Filax bounded up to lick Jo's and Will's hands. Will ruffled his fur.

'Good dog,' he said.

Selene smiled and gestured towards the doors, her hands leaving a wash of stars trailing in the air behind them. The doors swung open.

'Sweet dreams,' she said with an encouraging smile. 'Sleep tight. Don't let the bedbugs bite.'

8

A dragon calls

The Temple Bar dragon flew in low over the buildings to the east of the forecourt that separated the portico of the British Museum from the road in front. The frozen soldier-statues had been cleared away, and the only figures now standing there were knots of frozen people, glowing as if coated with the blue frost.

He landed without a bump, going from flying to walking without even the hint of a jolt. He strode confidently, straight up the steps, and walked towards the large double doors that barred the entrance.

He tried to open them. They stayed shut. He rattled the handles. Nothing moved. He raised his talons, bunched them into a tight metal fist and clubbed imperiously on the doors, three times.

Then he stepped back and listened for any movement from inside.

Within the museum, in the Egyptian Sculpture Gallery the lioness-women looked at each other. Bast lay sleeping beneath the pool of blue light in the deep man-shaped depression at the centre of the sarcophagus. The sound of three more knocks echoed across the Great Courtyard.

The look they exchanged now was more urgent. One nudged another and the nudgee passed it on to the next one. It was clear they were all trying not to be the one who woke Bast.

Three more knocks and then a low roaring noise, like a wind.

This new noise broke the spell.

It would, it appeared, have to be investigated.

Two of them left the others and walked out. As they threaded through the unmoving crowd of visitors they saw a new and different light beginning to glow from within the entrance hall, and they hefted their sticks and picked up the pace, jogging towards it.

'It' was the glow of wildfire-heated metal.

Outside the heavy doors the Temple Bar dragon had got tired of waiting. He was now *reasonably* calmly breathing fire on the doors, heating the metal so that it popped and crackled as it became red-hot and began to shimmer in the heat. It was a very controlled thing, almost surgical in its precision.

Inside the doors the lioness-women saw the metal beginning to glow, and one turned and ran back to the Egyptian Gallery.

The front runner skidded to a halt, gulped, then leaned over the sarcophagus and reached down with her stick, hesitating for an instant before poking the sleeping Bast.

The others all stepped another couple of paces back, looking at the would-be poker with a mixture of apprehension and respect. The poker looked back at them, shrugged and was about to jab the cat when Bast's eyes snapped open, and one sharp-clawed paw lashed out and stopped the stick.

WHAT WAKES ME?

The lioness-women looked out of the gallery towards the main door.

Before their eyes could catch up, Bast had sprung out of the blue bath and was streaking towards the growing red glow at the front of the museum.

The lioness-women caught up with Bast at the entrance. She sat calmly in front of them, tail flicking slowly back and forth, just as if she was a normal cat basking in the welcome heat of a fireplace. She did not appear a bit concerned.

On the outside of the doors the Temple Bar dragon

continued to breathe fire as he approached the doors – now almost white-hot – and reached forwards, pushing the handles with both talons.

This time the metal of the locks buckled and bent and snapped, and the doors opened wide.

From within it was like the blast doors to a furnace opening. The entire giant rectangle of the doorway was a billowing wall of flame that uncannily held the shape and pattern of the door's panelling for a moment, like an impression made in molten red, yellow and purple plasticine. Then it broke up as the black jagged shape of the Temple Bar dragon stepped through the standing wall of fire and looked down at the cat.

The cat held its ground, though its tail stopped moving.

The dragon looked around the Great Courtyard, the frozen schoolchildren, the tourists, the lioness-women hanging back, but already fanned out, as if waiting for an order to attack. He chuffed out a grunt of smoke that was definitely unimpressed.

WHAT DO YOU WANT?

Bast's voice was everywhere. The dragon did not speak, or if he did it was not at a frequency normal ears could catch. He looked at the cat as he walked past it, and some kind of communication passed between them.

I DO NOT KNOW ANYTHING ABOUT A DRAGON'S SHIELD.

The dragon stopped in the centre of the courtyard and looked back at the cat.

NOR DO I CARE.

The dragon cocked his head to the right.

I DO NOT CARE FOR THE SHIELD THAT IS LOST.

The dragon cocked his head to the left.

I DO NOT CARE THAT MIDNIGHT WILL PASS AND YOUR PRECIOUS MINION WILL BE MAIMED FOREVER BECAUSE IT HAS NO SHIELD TO MAKE IT COMPLETE.

The dragon did not move. He did not move in that very particular way that was a threat, because the not-moving was clearly a last chance of not moving, before he moved very drastically and finally for whatever was in front of him.

The cat read his eyes and then, without a shred of fear but a bucketload of contempt, slowly turned her back on the dragon.

NOR DO I CARE THAT YOU THINK YOU GUARD YOUR CITY.

The cat had turned, and her tail was now flicking back and forth again.

BECAUSE YOUR CITY IS LOST. YOUR CITY IS NOT YOURS. YOUR CITY IS MINE. AS ARE YOUR DRAGONS.

The Temple Bar dragon centred his head on his shoulders and cocked it straight backwards, this time like the hammer on a gun.

FEAR YOU?

Bast's voice dripped with contempt.

WHY WOULD I FEAR A DRAGON? A DRAGON IS NO MORE THAN A WINGED CROCODILE THAT VOMITS FIRE. FIRE CANNOT HARM ME, AND I HAVE SLAIN ENOUGH CROCODILES TO DAM THE NILE ITSELF. CROCODILE MEAT IS SWEET AND LEAN. YOU ARE AN OVERGROWN LIZARD WITH DELUSIONS OF GRANDEUR. **BUT I AM BAST!**

And with that the cat spun and hissed at the dragon, seeming in that moment to grow in size, although it was the voice that did that, cracking like a thunderclap.

YOU WILL BOW TO ME!

The dragon did not bow to anyone. Ever. So he snapped his head forwards like a whiplash, spitting fire instead, a great roiling billow of twined flame, jetting towards the cat.

Bast hissed, showing a snarling mouthful of teeth as her eyes flashed blue.

The wildfire hit a barely invisible wall that the cat had projected in front of herself, a wall made from magic and blue light and held in place by the intensity of hatred in its hiss.

Fire splashed sideways, trying to find a way round the impenetrable blue-light wall, as the cat and the dragon circled each other, one blasting wildfire, one hissing out a force-field, pivoting round the point where the unstoppable fire met the immovable light.

YOU CANNOT KILL ME.

Bast's voice echoed off the stone walls of the courtyard.

They continued to move, each straining to get closer to the other, unable to do so, like magnets repelling like from like.

THEY TRIED TO KILL ME LONG AGO.

The dragon redoubled the intensity of the flame-burst, clearly trying to drown out Bast's voice. The light wall held as the cat pushed back.

THEY COULD NOT. SO DO YOU KNOW WHAT THEY DID?

The dragon snarled.

THEY IMPRISONED ME.

The dragon snarled louder.

DO YOU KNOW WHAT I DID?

The dragon's chest expanded as he sucked in another lungful of air to fuel the fire he was spouting.

I DID THIS!

The cat sprang backwards, taking the blue wall with her. The dragon stumbled onwards. And then the cat leapt forwards, high in the air, up and over the dragon. And as she arced, the dragon shot flame at her.

But as the cat arced above the dragon, so did the wall. And when the cat landed, the wall stayed in an arch above the dragon.

The dragon whirled, trapped beneath a span of his own flame, and then before he could think straight, the cat streaked around him in a circle. The enraged dragon tried to roast the cat with his fire, but Bast the Mighty, Bast the Huntress, Bast the speeding bronze cat was closing the circle by dragging the wall of blue light around the dragon.

As she completed her circuit she stopped dead, suddenly as docile as a domestic cat again, and sat down, beginning to groom herself with a series of pointedly disinterested licks.

The dragon roared in a final desperate shriek of realisation.

Bast paused and looked up.

I LEARNED: WHAT YOU CANNOT KILL, YOU TRAP.

The roars of frustration began to change to something closer to pain. The dragon was penned within a dome of blue light, but the inner walls were rolling arcs of wildfire swirling about him on all sides.

Bast had won.

The dragon was imprisoned within a ball of his own fire.

Sometimes hell is other people. Sometimes you make it yourself. This was one of those times.

And it wasn't pretty.

9

Safe haven

Will and Jo had found the door to the hotel stairs tucked behind the elevator lobby, and were heading upward as Filax led the way.

'We must never split up again,' Will said as they climbed. 'Never.'

'We won't,' she said. 'I promise not to go stomping off in a huff again.'

'No,' said Will. 'Seriously, Jo. I give you my word. Whatever happens from now on, we stay together and we get through this together.'

She smiled at him, trying to take the edge of the tension they were both feeling. He stuck out his hand.

'We stay together and we get through this together,' she said, clasping his hand. They both gripped hard and shook.

On the second-floor landing they passed the rigid figure of a harassed-looking room-service waiter transfixed mid-step as he ran upward holding a single fork like an Olympic torch in his right hand.

They exchanged a look. Jo waggled her eyebrows.

'Weird,' she said.

'If we do get separated—' he started.

'Seriously, Will,' she said. 'I promise. My word. Cross my heart and all that stuff. We're not going to split up again.'

'I know. But remember the 7Ps,' he said. 'They still apply. Of course, we'll stick together, but if things DO go pear-shaped again, we just meet back where we left Mum. Coram's Fields. By the car. OK?'

She smiled back at him.

'OK. Good thinking, Batman.'

When they got to the fourth floor they had to move a loaded room-service trolley to get in the door. Will looked back down the stairwell to the waiter.

'Ah. He must have forgotten the fork,' he said.

'Yeah,' said Jo, eyeing the food on the trolley, her attention particularly focused by a large and glistening slice of dark cake, the kind her mother called Devil's Food Cake, and her father called Death-By-Chocolate.

She had a stab of memory, her parents sitting with them at the kitchen table, in the warm glow of candlelight from a birthday cake. And they'd all been laughing at how much of the chocolate cake had got onto Will's face instead of inside him. Then one thing led to another and her father had ended up daubing cake on her mother's nose and – well, it was just a good memory.

And then she thought of her mum now, cold and alone and unmoving somewhere in the frozen city, and suddenly the slice on the trolley didn't seem so tempting.

'Come on!' said Will, ahead of her. 'This looks great.'

He was already standing in the open door to a large corner room. She turned from the suddenly resistible cake, and followed him in.

It was, as Selene had promised, a very lovely room and certainly luxy. There were two large beds, and they had the kind of super-comfortable mattress that was firm enough to bounce on, but with a soft topper under the sheets that felt like the bed was not just gently holding you but would hug you and keep you safe as you slept. In short it was just what Will and Jo needed.

'These are really good beds,' said Will, falling back and spreadeagling himself on the one closest to the door.

Jo clicked on the light in the bathroom.

'Wow,' she said. 'It's like in a film.'

He rolled off the bed and peered in over her shoulder.

'Shower and a bath,' he said, looking at the pale marble and the clean modern lines of the space. 'And two loos.'

'That's not a loo,' she said. 'That one's a bidet.'

'A bee-what?' he said.

'Bidet,' she said.

'What's it for?' he asked.

Filax pushed in between them and nosed his way to the lavatory.

'No!' said Jo sharply.

'What?' said Will.

'He's thirsty,' she said, and stepped into the room. 'He was going to drink out of the lav.'

She pulled a lever and turned a tap, and the bidet began filling up. Filax looked at her, and then licked her hand. Strangely, the pale marble tongue felt soft and warm – and wet. He then began lapping at the rising water in the bidet.

'It's not really a dog bowl, is it?' said Will.

'Not really,' she agreed, ruffling her hand in the dog's mane, which was, again uncannily, both marble and as soft as real fur. 'But it works well as one, doesn't it? I'm thirsty too.'

'Minibar!' said Will. 'There'll definitely be a minibar in a posh hotel like this.'

They left the dog happily lapping up water as if he hadn't had a good drink for centuries, and went back into the room. The small fridge was hidden under the desk behind a door. It swung open revealing cans of sparking water, mineral water and a lot of tiny bottles of whisky, vodka and gin. There were also chocolate bars and jars of nuts.

'Jackpot!' said Will, grabbing a Coke and a chocolate bar and sitting on the end of the bed. Glancing at the widescreen TV fixed to the wall, he picked up the remote and clicked through endless channels of glitch: every programme was freeze-framed at the moment the rest of London had stopped. It was a tantalising series of images, teasing fragments sent to taunt them by showing what normal used to look like. He hadn't realised how used he was to screens giving him information or distracting him until it had stopped. In a similar way to his dead phone, it felt like he'd lost a sense, not a major one like sight or hearing, but one you don't immediately notice has gone, like smell or taste.

'Shame the TV doesn't work,' he said. 'That's a monster screen.'

Jo was sitting back on her bed, having taken some nuts and a chocolate bar for herself. She unpopped a can of Coke and took a long drink. She realised she felt as thirsty as Filax had been.

'You wouldn't be able to watch anything,' she said. 'What do you think would be on? You wouldn't be able to concentrate anyway.'

'It'd take my mind off things,' he said.

'You're obsessed with screens,' she said. 'Mum's right.'

'I'm not,' he said, chomping on a mouthful of chocolate.

'You are,' she said. 'I mean, this could be the end of the world and you want to watch TV? How responsible is that?'

'I'm not being irresponsible,' he said. 'I'm just saying! It'd be nice to not think about all this. Just for a bit. It's making my head buzz and fizz like it's going to overheat and explode. TV would be boring and normal. Just five minutes of boring and normal would probably be as much good as . . .'

And here he yawned hugely, immediately and treacherously, giving the lie to what he was about to say.

'. . . probably as much good as a sleep.'

She looked at him.

'Stop getting at me about screens,' he said. 'Right now that's as stupid as me – OK, I admit it – that's as stupid as me wanting to watch some crap TV show.'

Silence hung between them for a while. He found he was unconsciously rotating the scarab on the string round his wrist, and stopped again.

'OK,' he said. 'We're going to stick to the plan about Mum and her scarab. We'll go there when it's light. Without an armed escort. Maybe get Selene to fly us there.'

Another thought hit him. 'Maybe if we put it on a frozen statue, like the Fusilier, the spell would break like it did with you and me? Maybe we could do that? Maybe that would make him move and talk again?'

One of Jo's eyebrows twitched up in a way he normally found annoying because it was usually a sign she was about to say something snarky at his expense.

'Or we could go now,' he said a bit uncertainly. 'It's worth a try. A third scarab would definitely be cool, yeah?'

'That's a totally brilliant idea. Seriously. But you look as exhausted as I feel,' she said, wrong-footing him, which was almost as annoying as snark. 'Sleep would be better.'

'OK,' he said. 'We'll do it in the daylight. But one of us should stay awake and keep guard.'

He yawned again. A real jaw-cracker. 'I'll do the first bit, then I'll wake you. Say an hour?'

She looked at him. 'Will,' she said. 'You're kidding, right? How are you going to stay awake?'

He pointed at the mini kettle and the tray next to the small fridge. 'I'll make a coffee.'

'You hate coffee and you don't need to anyway,' she said. 'Selene said she would guard us. And we have Filax.'

There was a bump and a lurch on her bed as the large dog climbed up on it. He padded round in a tight circle, as if settling the covers to his own particular satisfaction, and then dropped into a curled position at the end of mattress. He looked at them both and then rested his great head on his shaggy paws, staring right at the door.

'See?' she said, leaning forwards to stroke him. 'Dog's got our backs.'

'I'm still going to stay awake,' said Will. 'You sleep first.'

'You're so stubborn, Will,' she said sleepily. 'But please yourself.'

And she closed her eyes. She heard him crinkle the

paper of his chocolate bar and throw it into the bin. Then she heard him rattling the cups and sachets and turning on the mini kettle.

'I can mix hot chocolate with the coffee,' he said, sounding pleased. Realising his mother had a scarab that might help had really cheered him. They weren't thrashing any more. 'Won't taste so foul.'

'That's a mocha,' she said. 'Or maybe a mochaccino.'

'A mochaccino it is,' he said.

She felt the comforting weight of the dog at the end of the bed, and stared at the inside of her eyelids, waiting for the slumber that was very insistently tugging at the hem of her consciousness to pull her down into what she very much hoped – but secretly doubted – would be a deep and dreamless sleep.

She heard the kettle begin to rumble and chunter, and then, after a bit, click and ping itself off. She lay there, anticipating the pouring noise and the clink of spoon on china as Will stirred his improvised coffee and chocolate cocktail, but he must have been under the impression she was asleep and had decided not to wake her by making the noise.

He was OK, Will. He was one hundred per cent boy, and that had its inbuilt limitations, of course. But though she would never let herself be caught telling him this, he was, in her book, as good as it gets. Deciding not to wake her was kind. He was brave and he was kind, and that combination of qualities was one she and her girlfriends valued. Boys loved being brave, of course. Every day, every boy seemed to be told they should be brave and tough and all that. But none of them seemed to think being kind was particularly important. Not that all the girls she knew were kind, far from it. Girls could be worse than boys. They could leave wounds with their tongues that would last much longer and do more harm than the thumping boys occasionally gave each other. Kindness was seen as a sort of wussiness, when Jo knew it was in fact an even more valuable virtue than bravery. She decided to tell Will this, and let him know she hadn't gone to sleep yet so he could make his drink.

She opened her eyes.

'It's OK,' she said. 'I'm still awake.'

He said nothing. She turned on her side to look at him.

He was fast asleep, head awkwardly cricked against the headboard, an open packet of hot chocolate in his hand, on the very point of spilling into his lap.

'Idiot,' she smiled, feeling a warm flush of affection for him as she leaned across the gap between the beds and slid it out of his grip, laying it on the bedside table.

He murmured and scrunched down the bed, straightening his neck as his head found the seductive squishiness of the pillows.

So the plan reversed itself, but not on purpose.

Will slept, and Jo did not.

10

The London Pride

The dragon from whom Will had taken the shield, the one that had been impaled on the railings at Coram's Fields, was now back on his rightful plinth. His brother or sister dragons (and deciding which sex a dragon actually is is quite a tricky subject, and one upon which your average dragon is more than usually sensitive) had replaced him just before midnight. The flame damage had cured itself, the humiliating line of holes where the iron spikes had pierced him had disappeared, and everything – almost everything – was right with his world.

He felt a bit dopey, as if he had woken from a long but not very restful sleep. He scratched his head and looked around. He saw the wide sweep of the Embankment and the river beyond. He saw the frozen cars, buses and people, which he remembered from before he had been melted by that unpleasant human child, the one who had oddly NOT been frozen like the rest of them. He snarled at the memory and his talons flexed and his fangs gnashed together with an unpleasant SKREEE of metal on metal. He turned round, then back again, padding and scraping his feet on the plinth, like a dog trying to make its bed comfortable.

Something was wrong. But he was still too fumbled up in his mind to work out what it was.

'Where's your shield?' said a very calm, very deep woman's voice.

He knew the owner of the voice. It was one of the two Sphinxes from the other side of the road, close to the river by Cleopatra's Needle. They had huge bodies, lion-shaped and the size and heft of bull elephants. But their heads were wholly human, smooth, beautiful and wearing Egyptian headdresses, like pharaohs. Their faces were so beautiful and calm that their sex was as hard to pin down as the dragons', but for entirely different reasons.

The dragon didn't much like the Sphinxes. There were several reasons for this. Firstly, they were both terrible know-it-alls who never did anything as simple as responding to a question with an answer. Instead they either replied with another question (which was frustrating) or a riddle (which made the dragon feel stupid).

Secondly, the Sphinxes confused the dragon, because on the one hand statues based on people were Spits, and on the other hand sculptures and carvings based on non-human things (like dragons or gargoyles or animals) were Taints, and there was a clear line of mutual suspicion and occasional outright conflict between the two groups. Sphinxes, half human half lion, blurred the clean line between the two camps and that was what baffled the dragon.

'Your shield?' repeated the Sphinx. It had stepped off its plinth and was crossing the road towards the dragon. It came to a parked car, and it was so large that instead of going around it, it was able to step right over it, the taut bronze curve of its chest and belly clearing the roof easily. 'I'm sure you had a shield. Big metal one; silver, with a rather large red cross painted across it?'

'You did,' said the other, following its sister (or brother). 'You were very proud of it. You held it up in front of you. Protecting the city.'

The two Sphinxes weren't quite the same. There was a nice one and a not-so-nice one. The not-so-nice one had been damaged a long time ago in an explosion, and the dragons had decided among themselves that this is what had made it tetchy, and a bit dangerous. It was, however, the one that was felt to be more on their side than the calmer, undamaged one that was (though they'd never say it to its face) a little bit more human.

'You look odd without it,' said the other. It had an unusual blue light in its eyes, as blue as the glowing frost covering the frozen people in the street around them. 'Lopsided.'

'And confused,' added the first one. The dragon looked closely at it and saw it was the nicer one. Its eyes, interestingly, were not blazing with blue light like the other's.

The dragon looked down at his front talons and saw they were right. What was missing was so big, so much a part of himself that he hadn't noticed, because it didn't seem possible that it wasn't there, clenched between his claws. The shield. The wretched boy had stolen his shield and used it against him.

The dragon felt stupid and felt naked. He snarled in frustration. He felt something else too, not just unprotected and missing something in his talons: he felt strange in his head, tugged at, compelled, and . . .

He didn't know the words. He looked at the Sphinxes. The closest one looked straight back, as if it could read the dragon's mind. Maybe it could. The dragon decided he wasn't going to give it the satisfaction of asking what it saw.

'You heard the call,' said the not-so-nice one. 'Even if you are still too fuggled from being healed at midnight to know you heard it. We are bidden to the Museum.'

'I will not go,' said the first Sphinx. 'I do not feel the compulsion.'

'I do,' said the other. 'It speaks to the part of me that does not think. It speaks in an old, strangely familiar voice. I shall follow that. I shall see what I shall see.'

'And I shall stay,' said the first Sphinx.

They both looked at the dragon. Now they had mentioned it, he realised that there was a magnetic tug drawing him towards the distant museum.

'You hear it. It calls you,' said the not-so-nice Sphinx. 'I can see it in your eyes.'

And just for a moment the dragon could see his own reflection in the shiny bronze of the Sphinx's headdress, and he could see it in his own eyes too: a cold blue light, as chilly and eerie as the frost-fire in the Sphinx's own eyes.

'Walk with me,' said the Sphinx. 'Maybe we will find you a shield on the way.'

Even when saying something encouraging it managed to sound like a sneer.

They headed north together, through the dark and cavernous streets. The unmoving people they passed were glimmering blue as ever, like luminous stalagmites leading the way along the bottom of deep city canyons from whose sides rows of mostly unlit widows looked down blindly on them.

As they made their way out into Trafalgar Square the dragon saw more movement, and realised they were joining a silent procession of all the animal statues in the city, who were being pulled in the same direction. The four huge lions from around the base of Nelson's Column were already gone, but there was no shortage of other lions, in stone, marble and metal, streaming northwards. There were many horses, and there were unicorns. There were lionesses and sheep and goats, and there were bulls and cows and cats. By the time the procession coming up from the river had wound north to the junction with Oxford Street and mingled with the flow of statues from the west, there were also elephants and buffalo and camels and several species of gazelle.

On the corner of Tottenham Court Road the Sphinx stopped and looked pointedly at a man holding a large stout sign above his head. On the plus side it was, the dragon had to admit, sort of shield-shaped. On the other hand it announced 'GOLF SALE LAST CHANCE!!!' in huge neon-green letters. Happily, the dragon could not read, so was able to hop across the stream of animals and snap the handle of the sign clamped in the frozen man's grasp, tucking the shield comfortably in his front talons. It was not the same as a real shield, but it helped, in much the same way as a stick can help when you're limping. It's better than being stuck, but not as good as real walking.

By the time he got back into the flow of the eerily silent cavalcade, the dragon was able to see clearly that there was also no shortage of dragons. In fact, as they turned into Bloomsbury proper and began to get close to the museum itself the dragon realised *all* the dragons in the city must be there. And as it looked out over the great herd of beasts beginning to filter into the open space in front of the museum, he realised what the other strange feeling was in his head: not only was he unable to see the Temple Bar dragon – his leader – he could not feel him either. Normally the dragons communicated silently, throwing thoughts back and forth to each other across the city, like an ongoing conversation on an open radio channel that they could all hear or chip into if they had news to share. The Temple Bar dragon, as the chieftain of their fire-breathing tribe, always rode in the back of their minds like a familiar, almost parental, warmth, the one voice in the conversation that was always there. And now it wasn't.

That feeling was gone. What was there instead was not quite emptiness, because the cold blue compulsion had taken its place, but it was a new and uncomfortable thing. When you have belonged, suddenly not belonging is a horrible feeling, like you are falling but don't know why.

The dragon felt just like that.

The assembly of animals was one of the strangest sights London had ever seen in its long history: the various species found each other without seeming to be told to do so. The more popular subjects for statues grouped into the largest phalanxes, so that meant the lions – and this included the Sphinxes – were the biggest block, then the horses, then the dragons and the unicorns, although since the unicorns were part of the heraldic shields carved all over the city they tended to be much less than full size, and so didn't take up as much room.

The horses were quite often saddled but riderless, and the dragon realised with a little smirk that there must be a lot of unhorsed Spits lying on their plinths and looking very undignified all over the city. At the other end of the size-scale there were snakes and rats and insects, and in one corner the twinkling glow of fireflies. In a big enough city with enough history and creativity, there's a good chance that someone will make a really surprising sculpture, and, sure enough, these fireflies had come all the way from the memorial to animals lost in war on Park Lane, accompanying a pair of overloaded mules and a proud-looking horse. The dog from the same sculpture was notably absent. In fact, no dogs were to be seen, a fact probably explained by Bast's feline dislike of anything remotely canine, or perhaps by the dogs' natural good sense in avoiding trouble.

As the loose squares and rectangles of the different animal groups settled into their positions in the front yard of the museum, like a series of regiments drawn up in parade review, the dragon felt something tickling his ankles.

He looked down and saw a stream of cats. Not stone cats or metal cats, but real cats – fat ones, thin ones, sleek ones and moth-eaten ones; tabbies and gingers, black cats and tortoiseshell, white ones and blue ones; some ridiculously fluffy like burst cushions, some dangerously sinuous and svelte. Bast the Mighty had released the real cats of London from the spell binding all living things, and had called them to form the feline squadron of what was, the dragon could now see, an army.

All the animals, real or sculptures, came in different shapes and sizes, but two things united them: they all looked out at the world with blue frost-fire blazing from their eyes. And every pair of those eyes was pointed at the front door of the museum, waiting for it to open.

There was a long-held breath of anticipation, and then the tall double doors slammed back to reveal a standing wall of blue light, through which stepped the lion-women. They formed an honour guard on each side of the door, and then Bast rode out between them on the back of the giant stone scarab, like a general standing on a tank. The scarab's thin insect legs skittered over the stone paving beneath the heavily armoured body as it walked to the edge of the steps, where it stopped and looked down on the massed ranks laid out beneath it.

A ripple of noise ran through the crowded masses

– a mixture of growls and purrs and low whinnies and quiet hissing. It was a strange noise, submissive and hungry.

Bast sat back on her haunches and raised one paw.

Something dropped heavily out of the sky and landed on her wrist. Horus the hawk folded his wings and added the unblinking blue disc of his eye to the cat's, looking out at the mass below.

I AM BAST. YOU ARE MINE. WE ARE MIGHTY!

The animals roared and shrieked and bellowed their approval. The dragons banged their shields on the ground, adding a clashing percussion to the cacophony. The dragon whose shield had been stolen went through the motions of banging his shield along with the other ones, but took care not to actually bang the replacement shield too hard. He had a feeling that if he did, he'd be holding a mangled mess of broken plywood, and that, in front of everyone, would make him look irredeemably stupid. And as we have already noted, stupid is a colour that dragons do not like.

THIS CITY MUST BE MINE. YOU WILL HELP ME. YOU WILL BE REWARDED. BUT FIRST YOU MUST FIND ME THE CHILDREN.

Bast looked around the yard.

TWO CHILDREN OF FLESH RESIST MY MAGIC. TWO UNFROZEN CHILDREN WHO STILL MOVE. FIND THEM. BRING THEM TO ME. THEN THE CITY WILL BE MINE. AND YOU SHALL BE REWARDED.

It might be that he was distracted, worrying about looking silly because he just had a flimsy wooden 'GOLF SALE' sign instead of a proper metal shield, but the dragon wasn't quite concentrating enough on being mesmerised by Bast's magic. He looked at the other dragons. Their eyes blazed blue and they were nodding and yacketing their fangs in approval. They all looked like him, not least because they had all been made in the same mould that had made him. But now, for the first time, he felt different. He felt lesser, because he had a pretend shield that probably wasn't fooling anyone, and it felt odd because though he was used to a voice in his head telling him what to do, it was the wrong voice. None of the other dragons seemed to mind this. So he decided he was broken, and that the boy had broken him, and so however hard all the others looked for the boy, he would be the one to find him and get his shield back and then bring what was left of the boy back here to prove his worth to the cat as soon as was dragonly possible.

So when Bast launched Horus back into the sky and roared:

GO, MY MIGHTY MINIONS! FIND THE CHILDREN WHO DARE DEFY US!

the dragon didn't move.

Every other animal burst into action and noise, and the ordered ranks erupted into a wild maelstrom of multi-specied mayhem, as if each statue or cat had decided to head off to all points of the compass at once. The dragon stayed very still. Thinking, then realising something, then trying very hard not to be seen to smirk at the secret knowledge he realised he alone had. And then, as the crowd thinned out as the creatures spread away into the surrounding streets, hoping to find the trail of the children more by luck and force of numbers, he stretched his stubby wings and rose carefully into the night sky.

What he had been thinking about was what he had observed just before he'd attacked Will and Jo the first time: they had been very interested in something. They had been prodding and poking at it and trying to move it. When he had attacked, they had tried to defend it as much as themselves.

And so while all the other animals went on the hunt

in one direction, with no clear plan, the dragon went in the opposite direction. Because what the children had been so concerned with was a person. And all the people apart from them were frozen. If that person they had been so interested in was still there, there was every chance that wherever they were now, they would return to her. The dragon knew about needing things: they had fussed with the woman and her things as if they really needed something, just like the dragon really needed his shield back. All he had to do was find the frozen woman and take her. He would bring her to Bast and be rewarded. Then he would join the rest of the dragons in the hunt for the boy, and for the shield itself.

11

Death-By-Chocolate

Jo was quite sure that with Selene and Filax on guard, there was no need for both of them to take turns doing the same job. And she could sense that her brain needed rest, as if the simple act of taking in every impossible and unfamiliar thing that had happened to them since the world stopped had physically exhausted it, like a muscle that had unexpectedly been called upon to run a marathon. She felt a dull ache at the base of her skull, and her eyes were scratchy with tiredness.

She closed them and tried to sleep. She focused on relaxing, and when that didn't work she focused on listening to any sounds she could discern in the great unmoving metropolis beyond the curtained windows. All she could hear was Will very nearly snoring, and Filax breathing.

The city was silent.

There is a thing that happens when you are really

tired that fools your brain into thinking you are hungry. Sapped of energy, and unable for whatever reason to replenish her batteries with proper sleep, Jo began to feel distinctly peckish. The chocolate she had eaten from the minibar had flooded her with a fast sugar-hit that had spiked her system, and now her body wanted more as she began to plummet down the steep slope on the other side.

She rolled quietly off the bed, shushed Filax, who turned an inquisitive eye on her, and opened the minibar. If she had been hungry for hard alcohol, champagne or macadamia nuts she would have been fine. She could have made out like a bandit, in fact. But she didn't. What she wanted, what the feeling-hungry-but-really-just-tired trickster in her skull was telling her she REALLY needed, was chocolate.

And the good news was that she knew exactly where to feed that need.

Death-By-Chocolate. One almost cartoony slice of cake sitting on a room-service tray just down the passage around the corner, by the lifts. She'd seen it going in, and now she wished she had paused to pick it up as they had passed.

Still, it was not far away, and would not take a moment to get it.

If she was not going to be able to get to sleep, there was no point in sitting awake and listening to her stomach rumble. It was greedy, yes, but after the day she'd had, she deserved a little something. Even as she had the thought she felt a tiny pang of sadness, small but sharp: her mother used to say the same thing every night about her glass of wine. She only ever had one at a time, and some nights she had none, but when she was tired, or when their dad had been out of the country with the army for a while, she'd wait until seven and then pour herself a glass of wine.

'Seven o'clock,' she'd say with a wink at the children. 'Been a long day. Time for a little something, I think.' And then she would get herself the single glass of wine, and sit with them as they had their evening meal. They would chink glasses, red wine for her, white milk for Jo (to help her broken bones heal) and clear water for Will. Then their mother would take a sip, lean back and let the knots begin to unwind. A little something, she would say, really hits the spot sometimes. Jo was thinking that that gleaming dark slice of chocolatey sinfulness down the corridor was just going to waste, and could so easily, so very pleasantly, be a little something for herself.

What harm could it do?

She held a hand up to Filax, whose ears pricked.

'Shh,' she said. 'Stay here. I'll be right back.'

Jo picked up her stick, took a glossy magazine from the table by the sofa and slid quietly out of the door. She looked carefully right and left, and saw there was no one there. The passage was dimly lit with tastefully concealed downlighters paced at one metre intervals. Maybe it was the lack of outside windows, but the whole space was somehow dampened and muted, as if the passage existed under water. She folded the magazine and wedged it under the door, keeping it open. She didn't want it to swing back behind her and shut her out.

She walked carefully down the thick carpet, which muffled her footsteps, and stopped at the corner. Just because this was perfectly safe and only going to take a couple of seconds didn't mean she was going to take anything for granted. She stood next to a door marked FIRE EXIT ONLY and poked her head round the angle in the corridor, expecting to see that delicious slice of Death-By-Chocolate waiting for her, only a few steps away – and instead saw it was gone.

Or if not entirely gone, at least half gone.

Or half eaten.

Or, in fact, half eaten and disappearing before

her eyes, still *being* eaten by a very hungry – and very gold – metal rat.

The rat stopped eating and lifted its head to look at her. It didn't look frightened. It looked . . . interested.

It was, she realised, one of the animals she had seen earlier on the front of the School of Hygiene and Tropical Medicine. There had been rats and fleas and ticks and . . .

The hissing noise from behind her reminded her what else there had been.

Cobras. She turned.

Midway down the hall, between her and the open door to their room, were two cobras. One slowly serpentining across the plush carpet towards her. The other turning to head for the bedroom.

'Will!' she shouted. 'Look out!'

And then things began to happen very fast, as things do when everything decides to go wrong all at once.

The cobra heading towards her stopped and rose on its tail, hood flaring in a menacing golden billow that framed its gaping mouth and the venomous fangs within.

The other cobra got low to the ground and accelerated into the bedroom, heading for Will like a bolt of molten lighting.

There was an enraged chittering from behind Jo, and the scrabble of claws on crockery as the rat leapt across the room-service tray and launched itself at her face.

She spun and flailed her stick at it, acting on instinct. She wasn't looking or aiming because there was no time to do either. She just struck out blindly. There were a hundred reasons why she should have missed, not least of which was that she was very bad at rounders, but this was the one time everything lined up perfectly. She felt the impact before she heard the thwack of stick on metal, and as the concussion passed from the stick into her hand and on up her arm, she saw the rat squawking as it twirled backwards through the air, paws spreadeagled and long whippy tail flailing like a broken helicopter.

She turned to defend herself from the cobra.

As it reared back to lunge at her, the doorway behind it suddenly filled with a big, fast-moving slab of hound-shaped marble that had the other cobra clamped between its teeth, shaking it like a terrier shakes a rat.

The cobra facing Jo struck towards her, and would have sunk its fangs in her had Filax not trapped its tail beneath one heavy paw that slammed down on it like a sledgehammer.

The cobra reached full stretch, so that it was a perfectly straight line, like a gold javelin pointed right at her face, its tail clamped and anchored to the floor by the dog at the other end.

Jo saw the teeth, and the angry eyes that seemed to hang in the air an inch from the end of her nose for the longest moment – and then she swore the snake made an 'Gulp!' noise as Filax scooted his paw backwards, shovelling the cobra so fiercely that it went flying away in the air behind him, twenty feet down the hall.

'Good—' began Jo, meaning to add, 'dog'.

She never got the time. Filax bounded forwards and barged her through the fire exit. She tumbled back and caught her hip painfully against the steps behind her, bringing tears to her eyes.

Scrambling to her feet, unable to think why the dog had done this – or even if he had meant to do it – she went to the door. She was about to open it when she heard the reason.

A lion roared.

Filax barked.

And then there was the shrowling, growling,

snarling maelstrom-sound of two big animals fighting for their lives.

She saw a blur of stone lion and marble dog pinwheel past the small square of safety glass in the fire door. The lion was trying to get at the dog's throat, and Filax was trying to shake it off. The lion clawed and snarled, and Filax spun and snapped, and then he hurled the lion off, trying to get at its throat instead. The lion shrowled in fury, and hooked at the dog with all four claw-tipped paws. Again the positions changed as the dog yelped and threw him off, as the attacker turned to defender and back again, with no let-up from either of them.

The fight threw them back and forth across the corridor outside, banging and crashing into the door with such force that it screeched on its hinges and Jo knew it would burst open at the next blow.

And so, with a final shout of 'Will! Get out of there!', she ran for the roof, hoping the fire door at the top would not be locked. Otherwise she was running into a dead end. And she had the nasty thought that if it was locked and things went badly with Filax, she might rather abruptly and unpleasantly find out exactly why it was they called it that.

12

False dawn

Will did not snap awake when Jo first yelled his name. He was buried beneath a mountainous slag heap of sleep that pressed down on him like the weight of the world. Instead he clawed himself back to consciousness, tunnelling upwards with a disoriented and rising panic, his mind jumbled, unsure whether he was dreaming or drowning: had he heard Jo shout or . . . was it in his imagination? He could so easily let go of the thought and just sink back down into the nice welcoming fug of sleep on this very comfortable bed if he had just imagined her voice . . .

The barking and roaring in the passage outside ripped him out of the blurry depths and unceremoniously dropped him hard onto the sharp edge of reality.

The room door was open.

Jo was gone.

Filax was fighting something in the passage with a

lot of bumping and thumping and snarling.

Will stopped in his tracks, halfway off the bed, paralysed.

He had to do something. His mind knew this. But his muscles didn't seem to be getting the message. Or maybe they were waiting for more detailed instructions.

He heard himself shouting.

'JO?'

So at least his voice was working. He tried to hear a reply through the noise outside.

'JO!' he shouted. 'Where are you?'

Filax and something fiercely muscled and made of stone windmilled past the open door.

Clearly someone was issuing orders to his muscles without him knowing it. Maybe there was an autopilot that took over in moments of crisis, a sub-routine that clicked into self-preservation mode when the conscious mind jammed. Whatever the reason, he found he had jumped off the bed and slammed the door shut.

Jo was gone. The thought had his gut churning in horror. He hoped she was hiding somewhere safe. He couldn't think why she might have left the room, or how something could have taken her from it without waking him.

For a brief moment he felt he should not have left

the dog outside to fight alone, but the feeling didn't last long: he knew he was no match for a lion, and would just get in the way. There was the banging noise on the walls and floor as the fight came barrelling back down the hall and past the door. He jammed his eye to the peephole and saw Filax had the lion by the scruff of its neck and was definitely holding his own. Luckily it was a Filax-sized lion, not a disturbingly huge one like the giant beasts that sat at the bottom of Nelson's Column in Trafalgar Square.

Filax fighting one of those colossal creatures would have been like a chihuahua challenging an elephant.

Will suddenly thought to check the bathroom, his heart leaping with hope, moving fast, wondering if Jo was perhaps frozen in her own fug of terror within the marble space. His heart fell with a lurch as he saw she wasn't.

He had to find another way out, so he could start looking for her, but he was trapped in the room. He had noticed there was a flat roof one floor below the window, and he thought that if he could get the window open he might be able to hang from the window ledge and drop safely onto it, making his escape down a drainpipe. It wasn't the best plan, but it was better than no plan. Except for the fact the windows probably didn't open. Maybe he could throw something through them, like a chair. Or maybe hitting it with the dragon shield would do the trick.

He pulled the curtains.

At first he thought it was morning, and he was seeing bright golden sunlight dappled through the leafy branches of a tree moving in the breeze.

Then his eyes focused properly.

There was no breeze. It wasn't quite morning. It was the flat, cold light of a drizzly pre-dawn. And the gold light was not coming from the sun, or anything as warm and comforting.

It was coming from the cold gilded metal of the skittering things pressed against the window, the giant bugs and ticks and mosquitoes from the School of Hygiene and Tropical Medicine, the partners of the snakes and the rats. They were pressed against the glass, just like moths trying to get into a well-lit room at night.

But they were, of course, bigger than moths. They were bigger than soup plates, and they were not hungry for the light within the room, which was dim. They brought their own light. And as he stared at them, at the way the mosquitoes whirred their wings and jabbed at the glass, seeing how hard they could hit it before

107

either it broke or they knocked themselves out, he realised that they were not just hungry. They were angry. He couldn't have explained it rationally, but they gave off a wild and furious energy as they rattled at the glass.

There was something extra unsettling about their malice, something insectile and alien and wrong. It did more than frighten him. It made his skin crawl, like he was itching from the inside and he couldn't scratch the feeling away.

Suddenly, opening the window seemed like the single very worst idea in the whole world.

One of the giant mosquitoes flew backwards and hung in the air, three metres out, just like someone taking a run-up to barge open a door, and then flew forwards at speed, ramming the window.

There was a harsh crack, but the window was made of toughened glass and it held. Will found he had instinctively raised the dragon shield to protect himself, which was strange because not only was it an entirely unconscious gesture but he also had no memory of having picked it up. The self-preservation autopilot seemed to be working overtime.

He yanked the curtains shut.

There was another sharp crack from behind them.

'Jo,' he said, voice crackling with worry. 'Where are you?'

13

Up and out

Jo was boosted up the stairs by such a surge of fear-fuelled adrenalin that her bad leg didn't hurt at all. Or if it did, the pain had got pushed so far down the list of things to be paid attention to later that it made no difference. It was only when she hit the cross-bar that opened the exit to the roof, clunking it forwards and making the door spring open, that she felt her knee spasm and lock up as she jarred to a halt

'Ouch,' she winced, and bent to rub it. Then she remembered the mayhem that might at any moment come bounding up the stairs behind her, so she took a moment to slam the fire door shut, and leaned back on it, getting her breath.

Her hot face was immediately cooled by the rain driving down out of the grey pre-dawn sky. She took a couple of deep breaths, and then checked the roof for any new threats: it was flat and empty, covered in rain-slick chips of gravel. There was a skeletal railing that ran around the perimeter, blocky air-conditioning units that looked like inside-out refrigerators, and some skylights.

Thankfully there were no lions or dragons or cobras or rats, golden or otherwise. There was just wet grit and the unsightly working bits of buildings that get piled on the top of modern buildings, the stuff no one is meant to see from the street.

Jo wrenched her mind into gear: she was, for the moment, safe: wet, shivering and definitely twinge-y in the leg, but temporarily safe. Temporarily was the problem: she knew she had to get back to Will, or get Will back to her, and there was only one way she could think of doing it.

Selene.

Selene was on the front of the building. She was meant to be guarding it. So that meant the lion and the snakes and the rats had crept in elsewhere, perhaps around the back. So Selene might, she realised, not even know what was going on.

There was a thunderclap and a brutally swift flash of lightning, and then the rain just seemed to bunch up and redouble its efforts at drowning the city. Jo limped across the roof, feeling the fat raindrops beginning to pummel her head and shoulders, her feet dragging across the gravel.

She got to the front of the building and gingerly looked down into the street.

It was empty. Or rather it was full of unmoving people who glowed blue and ghostly in the gloom of the downpour, but there was no sign of Selene where she should be, on guard on her plinth overlooking the front entrance to the hotel. No Selene. No help. Just plinth.

'Great,' said Jo through gritted teeth. 'Just gr—'

The word died on her lips, unfinished. Below her she saw two large bronze lions prowl lazily round the corner, threading between the frozen people, low to the ground, their tails twitching sinuously – unmistakably hunting. They stopped at the front door to the hotel and leaned gently forwards, nostrils flaring. One of them jammed its muzzle to the gap beneath the glass door and worried at it, sniffing air in noisily, as if trying to inhale whatever was inside, like a giant feral vacuum cleaner.

The second lion raised its head to look upwards. Jo wound her own head back so fast she heard bones click; she didn't want to be seen. There was no way the lion could jump even a quarter of the way up to the roof, but she didn't want it to spot her, nor did she trust herself to look into its eyes.

Will. He was trapped in the room, unaware that there were lions in the building, and more than one by the look of it. She had to warn him.

She scrabbled back and edged around the perimeter of the roof. There was no easy way off the building that she could see, but she didn't want to retrace her steps down those stairs. Her heart was still thudding hard, trying to punch its way out of her ribcage, and she could hear herself panting hoarsely. She shut her mouth and tried to calm herself by breathing through the nose.

She realised she might be able to shout down to Will and warn him. She quickly jogged across to the back of the building and looked gingerly over the edge, trying to remember how many floors she had run past so she could work out which window was his.

She didn't need to work it out. It was clear. The huge gold bugs fluttering around the window were the big giveaway. From outside she could hear a whirring and a high-pitched whine that Will – inside the room and muffled by the double glazing – had been spared. She saw the gilded mosquitoes, big as falcons, taking it in turns to bash themselves against the glass. Every time they hit, all the raindrops bounced off and fell outwards in a fine mist.

She withdrew her head and took a deep breath to calm herself, because her mind really did feel like it was about to collapse into hopeless panic. She tried to find something to hold on to. The thing they'd said as they shook hands back on the stairs came back to her.

'We stay together and we get through this together,' she said out loud. She heard herself and suddenly knew she had a choice: she could be saying that to torture herself with how hollow the words now sounded. Or she could decide to live up to them. And living sounded better than torture.

'OK,' she said quietly, as she leaned on her stick. 'Lions at the front, bugs at the back. Let's see what happens at the side . . .'

She was halfway across the width of the building when she found out. First there was a whomping sound, like helicopter rotors in slow motion.

That stopped her in her tracks.

Then, through the rain that was now pelting down like stair rods, she saw something rise into view from beneath the edge of the building.

First a dark puff of steam, then wingtips that disappeared as the dragon beat downwards, raising its spiny head above the parapet. Then the full and dreadful span of wings as it clawed itself higher into the pelting downpour. The muscular tail that hung beneath it lashed into view and it bounced up and forwards over the railing and landed with a thunderous crack on top of a big skylight, whose raised plinth gave it even more height above her, and added to the theatrical horror of its appearance.

It looked nastily pleased with itself, red tongue lolling out of a monstrously fanged smile. It was so busy enjoying the effects of its surprise appearance that it did not attack immediately, but stood there enjoying the moment.

She gripped her stick in both hands, ready to swing it in self-defence; she was surprised to find she was determined to go down fighting, no matter how futile that might be.

It didn't feel like she was being brave. It didn't feel like a choice at all. It was simpler than that: she had nowhere to run. She was done. All she could control was how she went. And getting all teary and blubbery would only add to the win for the dragon. And this dragon was not getting any more win from her. Giving it more win to gloat about would be . . . undignified.

'Come on then,' she said, voice gravelly with the

fear she was trying not to show. 'What are you waiting for?'

The rain beat down. It rat-tailed her hair and plastered her clothes to her back. It made the hot metal of the dragon's neck and chest steam and hiss, so that it had a kind of permanent ghostly ruff around its shoulders. It was in no hurry. It was wallowing in expectant gloat.

She had more time to think, then. She knew she could move quite fast, especially if she ignored the pain in her knee, but she really didn't think she could make it through the fire-escape door before the dragon snatched her with those savage talons, or crisped her with a blast of wildfire. But maybe if it leapt for her and she sidestepped it . . .

Maybe, just maybe, in the very short interval it took to turn itself round she might buy enough time.

So, in the extra moment the dragon's gloating allowed her, that became her plan. After all, it was at least something, and something is always better than nothing, and there was just the one dragon.

'Just the *one* dragon,' she said bitterly, laughing at herself. She could hear the hysteria rising behind her voice. It was, however, like football. She'd been good at football before she fell through the roof and had her leg pinned back together. And one thing she knew was that to avoid someone's tackle, you had to wait until they had committed themselves to it, and then you could move out of their way as their momentum worked in your favour and took them past you. She just had to make this thing move.

She knew how hopeless and unrealistic this was, but no realistic plans were occurring to her right now. She must look pretty silly, standing braced like some kind of rain-sodden ninja-samurai wannabe, legs apart, flimsy stick held two-handed like a sword, dwarfed and soaking. Maybe that was why the dragon was giving her such a very nastily amused look.

The situation was hopeless. But the nasty look was the last straw. It was unbearable. She felt anger spike through her fear, like a sudden explosion of heat needling behind the bridge of her nose. She knew this was her eyes getting red, and though the rain would likely hide any tears of frustration from the dragon, she was determined not to betray herself in front of it.

'COME ON!' she yelled, and stamped her leading foot closer. 'COME ON! WHAT ARE YOU WAITING FOR?!'

Dragons probably don't snigger, but the noise this one made definitely oozed quite a lot of smirk. As if to emphasise its power and to show it was in no particular hurry to barbecue her, it looked casually behind itself, and as her eyes were inexorably drawn after it, she saw precisely and terribly what it HAD been waiting for.

Another dragon, its silver-painted twin, rose from below the lip of the building with the same ominous whomping wing-thud and, in a movement that matched the first one so exactly that you might have thought their motions were rehearsed, it bounded forwards and landed next door to it on the raised skylight, with a similarly percussive crack.

The only difference between them was the shield it carried. It wasn't metal. It was plywood. And instead of a proud red cross it shouted 'GOLF SALE LAST CHANCE!!!' at her, in foot-high neon lettering. She didn't have the time to begin to wonder what that was about.

Both dragons looked very pleased with each other indeed. For about half a second. Then they turned to look at her instead.

One dragon was quite bad enough. Escaping one dragon was the wildest of wild long shots. But *two* dragons?

'Last chance?' she muttered to herself, looking at

the plywood shield. 'More like Game Over.'

She needed a miracle.

Perhaps if she could make them both attack at once she could dive *between* them and they might get tangled up as they tried to turn and chase her. Or maybe she should just get this thing started so it could all be over sooner.

Her mouth was too dry to say anything brave or clever, so she hefted the stick and stamped forwards another six inches.

The dragons looked at her. Then looked at each other. And then they definitely, DEFINITELY sniggered. Both of them.

Then they turned and looked at her and did something even worse.

The first dragon imitated her. It shuffled round so it was side-on, like she was, then it raised its stubby arms as if holding an imaginary sword, and then stamped its foot. Just like she'd done. The other one sniggered, wobbled its eyebrows and did exactly the same, adding a really demeaning wiggle of its bottom as it did so.

The other dragon emitted a gleeful and wheezy *'sheesh sheesh sheesh'* noise as it giggled at its friend's antics, and stamped its foot again.

Toughened glass can take a lot of punishment.

But it isn't indestructible.

One minute there were two dragons mocking and mimicking her. Then there was a loud splintering noise.

One of the dragons went 'Ulp . . . ?'

The other went '. . . Ook?'

And then the glass beneath their feet splintered and gave way, and gravity took over as they dropped straight down the light well beneath them, plunging out of sight as abruptly as if a mysterious hand had just erased them from the planet.

One hit its chin on the lip of the skylight with a surprised grunt of pain as it plummeted away, snapping its snout towards the sky and leaving a surprised puff of smoke hanging in the air, as a kind of exclamation mark.

Jo and Will's dad was a great believer in mulligans. Mulligans are do-overs. Playing table tennis, if you messed up your first serve, you were allowed one mulligan, which meant you started again. It was a family rule. And as a soldier he had expanded this rule to life in all its unpredictability, a large and unpleasant portion of which he had seen, and tried very hard not to bring home. All he did bring home was the positive

lessons this hard side of his work had taught him. 'Work hard, play hard, rest and eat when you can, don't worry about failing, just fail better next time – and when fate offers you a mulligan?' he would say. 'Grab it with both hands.'

The dragons falling through the skylight was the mulligan of mulligans and Jo grabbed it without thinking.

She spun and sprinted for the door, feet kicking spurts of rain-soaked gravel as she ran.

She leapt over the gaping skylight and caught a glimpse of the two dragons tangled together at the foot of a long and narrow light well. It hadn't given them quite enough space to unfold their wings, but just enough to get thoroughly snarled up with each other. She landed on the other side with a sharp pain in her knee that made her stumble and gasp.

Stumbling saved her because as she bent over, something gold buzzed over her head so close that she felt the whirr of its angry wings on the exposed back of her neck. She looked back and saw, with horror, that it was one of the golden mosquitoes.

That wasn't a real mulligan then.

Or if it was, it was the shortest one in history, more like a very dispiriting out-of-the-frying-pan-into-the-fire-flavoured-mulligan instead.

The mosquito hummed into the rain and curved back on itself, returning to the attack.

Jo raced for the door, running badly lopsided now, the pain pounding through her knee with each step. She heard the approaching high-pitched whine behind her and spun, whiffling her cane through the raindrops, missing the mosquito entirely. It passed her, looped back up into the sky and came back for the kill.

'Girl!' shouted a voice from behind her. 'Run to me!'

She snapped her head left.

Selene was hovering by the edge of the building, beckoning her.

Jo ran, hunched low, legs pounding, towards the open arms.

'Keep running and jump!' cried Selene, which confused Jo, but not nearly as much as the fact that as she heard the mosquito closing in on her again, Selene's own dragonfly wings whirred and misted the raindrops as she flew straight at her.

'Duck and then jump!' she yelled as she overflew Jo, missing her entirely. Jo craned her neck backwards and saw the goddess of sleep bring her hands together in a mighty double swat that sandwiched the mosquito and splatted it in a satisfying shower of gold.

'Jump!' shouted Selene.

Jo caught the note of worry in her voice and realised she was still moving forwards, too close to the edge of the roof to stop, too powerless to make the leap across the chasm of the alley between her and the next-door building. Her legs became desperate and disjointed as despite all this her body tried to stop her, and then her foot caught the low wall and tried to brake her forward momentum—

It was too little too late, and all she did was send herself into a flailing cartwheel out beyond the end of the roof, tumbling down into the rain-filled gulf of air beyond.

14

Dog gone

Man's Best Friend v. King of the Jungle is not even close to a fair match. Normally a dog would have no chance against a lion.

Luckily for Will, Filax was a larger-than-life sculpture of an especially fierce kind of hound, bred to defend herds of sheep and cattle against wolves and bears, whereas the lion that had crept into the hotel on the trail of Will and Jo was a half-life-size sculpture of a heraldic lion whose day job was propping up one side of a coat of arms and trying to look more decorative than the unicorn that leaned against the other side of the shield. It wasn't quite a *wild* lion: it was more of an indoor lion, carved for artistic effect, not built for speed and ferocity.

Filax had rather enjoyed dispatching one of the golden cobras, and he had tossed the other out of harm's way before engaging with the lion, so he was warmed up and ready for a scrap. Decorative though the lion might have been, it was still a lion, and the fight was quite evenly matched. The two animals turned into a whirling ball of marble and sandstone as they bit and slashed at each other. Filax's advantage was that he managed to get a grip on the lion's back, which meant that the lion's main advantage – the cruel talons on its paws – could not get at him in any substantially disabling way. If they had been fighting face to face it would have been a shorter conflict, because a lion likes nothing more than getting a grip with its forepaws and then slashing away with its back claws in a horrible disembowelling movement. If they'd been head to head Filax would have been scooped open like the kind of soft toy whose stomach Jo used to unzip and store her pyjamas in.

As it was, Filax – fierce, wise and lucky in the way that a lot of wise people (and dogs) seem to be lucky – kept the advantage by not letting the great cat get its claws in him. The lion did manage to scratch at his side, leaving gouges in the marble, and he did at one stage get a nasty bite in on his leg, but Filax's ferocity kept him too busy to do very much damage.

The roaring and romping up and down the corridor was the lion's primary tactic, hoping to scrape the tenacious hound off his back onto the side walls as he

126

passed. It wasn't a very effective tactic, though it was a noisy one, as its main effect was to either snap off or bend all the door handles along one side of the passage.

It was one of these door handles that was the lion's ultimate undoing, because as it reached the end of a particularly vertiginous dash down the corridor, trying to shake off the unwelcome piggyback passenger that had stapled itself to its shoulders by its teeth, it tried to stop.

Unfortunately it put its front paw down on the cylindrical metal of one of the broken door handles, which acted like the wheel of a roller skate and sent it hurtling forwards into the end wall, instead of halting it.

The lion knocked itself clean out. Filax felt it go limp between his teeth. He held on until he was sure, then let go and bounded back down the corridor to bark urgently at Will's door.

Will, on the other side of the spyhole, took a good look. The dog was panting excitedly and its tail was wagging. He took a deep breath and opened the door. A quick look right and left revealed a corridor sprinkled with door handles like fallen apples, an unmoving golden cobra and a similarly motionless stone lion stacked up against the far end.

Filax barked and tugged at the shield Will held in his right hand.

'OK,' said Will. 'I get it. Time to go.'

Filax thumped his tail and led Will to the fire-exit door.

'Do you know where Jo is?' he said.

Filax pawed at the door

Will pushed it open and began to head downstairs. Then he heard the noises from above, and felt the draught of the door open to the roof above him.

He heard Selene's throaty voice shout, 'JUMP!'

And without thinking he was pounding upwards three steps at a time.

'Jo!' he yelled. 'I'm coming!'

He got to the doorway at the very moment Jo went over the edge.

It was a sight that might well have stopped his heart dead in horror, but as it happened, the edge she went over was to the right, and his eye was whipped leftwards, following the starry transit of Selene howling across the roof, fighting a swarm of hawk-sized mosquitoes and super-sized flying bugs.

'Jo!' he shouted, looking round the wet, empty roof.

Selene heard him and for an instant caught his eye.

'Run!' she cried. 'She's gone!'

He was about to shout another question, when he saw one of the bugs take advantage of the way he'd distracted Selene from the fight, weaving between her protective cloud of star and fastening horribly on her face. She went rigid with shock, and then began to whirl in place, faster and faster until she was invisible in the centre of a spinning vortex of stars as she tried to hurl the bug off her face and keep the other attackers at bay beyond the defensive golden cyclone of which she was now the epicentre. Every now and then a mosquito or a bug would try and get through the gilded twister, only to be hit by one of the stars with a sharp, metallic impact that sent sparks trailing after the insect as centrifugal force knocked it clear of her.

Will never got to see if she managed to get the suffocating bug mask off her mouth, because one of the mosquitoes, turning away from her, saw him and recalibrated its target. It shot straight towards his head, and without thinking he leapt backwards, pulling the door closed behind him. He would have fallen straight back down the stairs, probably breaking his neck, but luckily Filax was right behind him and absorbed the impact, acting as a safety guard.

The mosquito hit with a loud chunk, and Will saw the door bow inwards with the impact. He almost expected to see the golden stinger pierce the wood.

Then he heard Filax bark, and turned to see the dog was pointing with his nose down the stairs.

'Oi,' hissed a voice from below. 'What you doing?'

He looked over the edge. Two floors down he saw Little Tragedy looking back up at him with his fingers to his lips.

'What?' said Will.

'Shh,' said Tragedy, beckoning him urgently. 'We're up to our unmentionables in bleedin' lions. That cat's got 'em all stirred up. We got to go. Wolfie's waiting in the kitchen, keeping an eye . . .'

15

Going Underground – part 1

Jo had cartwheeled off the roof into the narrow canyon of air that separated it from the next-door building, grabbing fruitlessly for handholds that didn't exist. She didn't even have time to inhale, let alone yell out in horror at the speed with which the hard floor of the alley leapt towards her, a strip of rain-soaked concrete full of sharp-edged things like dumpsters, bicycles and scooters. She just had time to feel two things – a sucking void of sadness in the middle of her chest that she was going to be snuffed out, and to hope she would be extinguished so fast that the pain wouldn't get to her brain before everything went black and silent forever . . .

She looked away from the ground and saw, for a miraculous instant, the last thing she knew she would ever see. And maybe because it was the last thing she'd ever lay eyes on, she saw it in unnaturally sharp focus, almost as if her eyes zoomed in on them – the fat raindrops beside her, falling at exactly the same speed as she was . . .

. . . and then the end came and hit her . . .

. . . and it did hurt, but the pain was more like being winded than smashed, and it was not at all terrible, and instead of black it was golden, and it wasn't silent either.

It said:

'Ooof! You're heavier than you look . . .'

It was Ariel. The golden girl statue from the Bank of England. The one Jo had last seen melted in half by an angry dragon. Midnight had obviously worked its magic on her as it had on the Fusilier, because here she was, as whole and as fast and graceful as she had ever been, swooping in low to catch Jo and save her life. For the second time.

'Gnaargh . . .' said Jo. Meaning to say 'thank you' but being too shocked and winded to get it out in an unsnarled version.

'And gnaargh to you too,' said Ariel. 'Now, hold on.'

Jo did as she was told. Her mind was still catching up with the good news that she wasn't a splat on the pavement, and her lungs had just managed to fill with their first full breath after the shock of being caught. It felt wonderful. Ariel flew low to the ground, turning right at the end of the alley and heading away from the hotel.

Jo looked back over her shoulder and saw two huge bronze lions the size of elephants nosing at the front door of the hotel.

'Will!' she gasped, her moment of elation disappearing instantly. 'He's in there. Stuck in the hotel.'

'Selene and Tragedy will get him out,' said Ariel. 'They'll bring him.'

'Bring him where?' said Jo.

'Here,' said Ariel, swooping up and over a double-decker bus full of frozen blue-tinged people staring vacantly past them. Jo's stomach lurched as if she was on a roller coaster. 'Tragedy had a good idea . . .'

Ariel landed beneath the well-lit canopy of a tube station and put Jo back on her feet. Jo staggered and realised that somewhere in the fall she had dropped her stick. She straightened up and grimaced.

'And where's Tragedy?' she said.

'He's back in the hotel with Wolfie.'

'Who's Wolfie?' said Jo.

'One of Tragedy's little gang. We were trying to warn you about the lions,' said Ariel.

'Bit late for that,' said Jo.

'I know,' said Ariel. 'We got rather surprised by them.'

'Thank you for catching me,' said Jo. 'I, er . . .'

'Think nothing of it,' said Ariel breezily, running her fingers through her hair. 'I thought you were the boy anyway.'

'Will,' said Jo.

'Yes,' said Ariel. 'Will. Though I should have caught you just the same if I'd known it was you, which, now I come to think of it, I did.'

She turned a smile on Jo that was evidently intended to dazzle and impress.

'I'm grateful,' said Jo. 'And I'm glad you're mended.'

'So am I,' said Ariel. 'It was very painful and uncomfortable, the whole dragon thing. I can't think why they are so stirred up.'

'Yes,' said Jo. 'And now there are lions.'

'Where?' said Ariel, the smile sliding off her face as she looked hurriedly around the street.

'No,' said Jo. 'Not here. Not now. I mean back there. You know. Everywhere. They seem to be hunting.'

'The London Pride,' said Ariel. 'That's what they are called. Every now and then all the lions get together and roam about, but they just do it for fun.

I mean, they don't normally hunt or attack things, not really, and if they do it's just for fun. Admittedly there are some deer statues and a couple of gazelle sculptures that they will stalk if they wander close, but they're awfully good sports about it. If they do catch them and bring them down they always drag them back to their plinths so they can be mended at midnight.'

'Not much fun for the deer,' said Jo.

'I suppose not,' said Ariel. 'But it's all done in good spirit; there's no malice in it. These lions aren't wild lions. They're London lions. You know. Fierce but polite. Normally . . .'

'But this isn't normal,' said Jo.

'None of it,' agreed Ariel. 'And is it your fault?'

'Why do you say that?' said Jo.

'Because you're the only people not frozen and the lions seemed to be hunting you. And the dragons don't like you . . .' She looked at her with a carefully raised eyebrow. 'No offence, but it is a tiny bit suspicious, isn't it?'

Jo wondered why when people said no offence they always followed it with something unpleasant that was a bit offensive.

'No, it's not us,' said Jo. 'We aren't affected by the

magic because we've got these scarab bracelet thingies that seem to be a talisman against it.'

'Bracelets,' said Ariel, suddenly interested. 'Oh, I do rather like jewellery. Show me.'

Jo held out the arm with the bracelet on it. Ariel reached out a slender gold hand.

'May I try it on?' she smiled.

'No,' said Jo, withdrawing her hand quickly. 'If I take it off I'll freeze like everyone else.'

'Oh, fine,' pouted Ariel, clearly more than a little piqued. 'I don't mind not trying it on. It's a rather grubby thing; really just a pebble on a string, isn't it? I expect if I was to wear jewellery it would look better to have something much bigger and more sparkly than that anyway.'

She began running her fingers through her hair again, suddenly preoccupied with carefully teasing it into an artfully tousled look as she looked at her reflection in the ticket-office window.

Jo's elation at Ariel's regeneration was beginning to subside slightly: she had forgotten how pleased with herself she always was, and how keen to share that assessment with anyone she was talking to.

'So what was Tragedy's good idea?' asked Jo.

'What?' said Ariel, primping a curl and smiling at

her reflection.

'You said he had a good idea?'

'Oh, yes,' she said. 'He thought the way to get around the city without the dragons seeing you was to go underground. On the Underground. I mean, through the tunnels. Because obviously the trains aren't working. And dragons don't go underground – at least I've never heard of them doing so – so the fact they can swoop around the sky looking for you wouldn't matter.'

Jo instinctively thought this was a bad idea. She was about to start listing the very many reasons why, beginning with the whole electrified-third-rail thing, but Ariel went on.

'He says you want to get back to your mother, and this does seem like a good and unusual idea. He's small but quite clever, for a boy . . .'

She stepped back, smoothing the material that rippled round her body as she admired her handiwork in the glass window. Jo still couldn't quite believe how little actual fabric there was, or work out how it always managed to stay eddying round her like a skein of golden smoke, no matter in what direction she moved.

Ariel caught Jo looking at her and smiled.

'You know, you could look perfectly nice if you did

something to your hair and wore a dress,' she said.

'Shut up,' hissed Jo.

'I was only—' began Ariel.

Jo just grabbed her and pulled her towards the escalators, ricocheting off the frozen people.

'Mind my arm!' screeched Ariel. 'You're hurt—'

'Shhh,' hissed Jo again.

But it was too late. The truck-sized lion she had spotted moving towards them through the windows of the red double-decker heard Ariel's screech and bounded round the front of the bus, heading straight for them.

16

Will, herded and hunted

Will and Filax followed Tragedy quietly down the stairs. As they went, they heard other noises in the building, the sound of big creatures patrolling the floors that they tiptoed past.

Tragedy held up a hand as they moved on down from the ground floor to the basement. They paused, holding their breaths, Filax tense and ready to pounce at whatever was snuffling noisily on the other side of the fire door, but whatever it was either didn't smell them or was unable to figure out how door handles worked, and it stayed shut. The noise moved away and they breathed again.

'Come on,' said Tragedy, and led the way down the last flight into the bright white light of the kitchen. It was a glaringly lit maze of efficient steel units and countertops, with a frozen cook stuck in the act of turning an omelette in a pan. He looked bored with his job.

'Jo,' said Will urgently. 'We've got to get Jo.'

'She'll be fine,' said Tragedy. 'Ariel was out there.'

'Zee little fraulein vent flyink off zee roof and tumbled through zee air like a rag doll,' piped an overexcited child's voice from the other end of the kitchen. 'Seriously, it vas completely highwire bananas! I thought she was goink to splat like a rotten tomato on zee ground, but Ariel caught her so zee Bob iss your uncle and no spilled milk to cry over.'

The head of a small boy made of dark bronze, just like Tragedy's, grinned round the corner. His face was more refined than the little imp's and his cheeks a little better fed, but the smile was just as puckish. He wore an old-fashioned wig with side-curls, and a perky little bow and pigtail at the back; he had a long jacket, a bit like a pirate's, with the ruffles of his shirt poking out of the cuffs, and more flounces tumbling over the high collar of the brocaded waistcoat he wore beneath it.

'What?' said Will, looking at Tragedy. 'Who's . . . ?'

There was so much adrenalin pumping through his system, swirling in with his fears for Jo and the overall rising tide of exhaustion that was threatening to drown him, that this new thing, this little boy in the wig with the flounces and the cartoony German accent was just not computing. Or at least if it *was* computing it was coming up with a big error message, and he did not know how to reboot his head and get back to normal. Maybe normal was now like the past, a place you can never go back to. The thought chilled him and he actually shivered, though that might have been the fight-or-flight surge of hormones flushing out of his system.

'Oh, that's Wolfie,' said Tragedy, as if that explained everything.

'And, er, what is he?' said Will.

'Well, he thinks he's a bit Austrian. Or German. Or both. He's not too fussy. Some of the statues say he's a child prodigy, and some say he's a *wunderkind*, which is why he talks funny, but I don't really know what either of those is, truth to tell.'

'I am a *wunderkind*!' giggled the boy. 'Everyone agrees. And maybe also I will be prodigy, though I don't know vot it is either, except it sounds fun!'

'He likes fun, does Wolfie,' said Tragedy.

'This isn't fun . . .' said Will, who was desperate to find Jo.

'I know,' said Tragedy. 'Hang on and I'll fill you in.'

And he quickly explained how he had been on the way back to meet Jo and Will when the animal statues had begun to step from the plinths and unpeel from the walls where they normally stood and stream towards the museum. He'd sent Selene, who he'd whistled out of the sky, to go and get them, while he went to fetch Wolfie.

'Because we need a secret weapon,' he added.

'And Wolfie's it?' said Will, voice dripping with disbelief as he stared at the boy, who must only have been nine or ten. He didn't look like a secret weapon.

'Just you wait,' said Tragedy. 'We get into a tight corner with them animals out there in the streets, Wolfie's going to buy you a lot more time than a couple of normal soldier-statues.'

'He doesn't look like a soldier,' said Will.

'Thank you,' said Wolfie, and bowed.

'You don't have a gun. Or even a sword,' said Will.

'No,' agreed Wolfie. 'I have better.'

And he raised his hand, which had been hanging below the counter so that Will had not been able to see what it held.

'A violin?' he said, choking. 'Are you serious?'

'I am better zan serious, my friend,' said Wolfie, winking at him. 'I told you: I am prodigy.'

Wolfie may have been a prodigy, and Tragedy may have believed he was a secret weapon, but Will noticed they both moved very slowly and silently as they eased out of the back door of the basement and crept down the alley.

The downpour was heavier now, and the glowing blue people on the street beyond the mouth of the alley seemed to acquire a haze around them as the driving raindrops refracted their light as they hammered past. It was the kind of rain that hits the ground so hard that it bounces back up your trouser legs and soaks your ankles. Within a few steps Will was drenched. He put his hoodie up and kept his right hand on Filax's back as they went along.

When Filax stopped, he stopped. A large silhouette of a lion slunk past on the street, backlit by the blue glow of the pedestrians.

Tragedy and Wolfie seemed to melt into the wall, and Will lowered into a crouch behind a parked scooter.

By the time the lion had moved on, Will's hoodie was so wet and heavy that it deadened his hearing and flapped on either side of his face like a pair of blinkers, severely narrowing his field of vision, so he pushed it back and resigned himself to getting thoroughly soaked. Creeping around with blinkers on seemed a suicidal thing to do in the circumstances.

He needed all his wits about him.

It took them five minutes to creep to the end of the alley.

What they saw there was dispiriting – four lions in view, and Selene, broken, lying across her plinth on the face of the hotel above the door, arms hanging lifelessly as a gold bug fluttered on her face. All her stars lay in a pile across the front doorway below, like discarded confetti. Will felt the familiar pang of guilt. Maybe she had succumbed to the bugs' attack because he had distracted her for that crucial moment. They turned back and took a further five minutes creeping back to where they'd begun.

'We're a bit bottled in,' admitted Tragedy. 'If bleedin' Ariel would come back she could fly us out of here. Dunno what she's up to.'

In the near distance they heard a lion roar with a ground-trembling blast of hunter's frenzy.

17

Going Underground – part 2

Ariel and Jo were, for an instant, paralysed with fear in the ticket hall of the Underground station. In two leaps the roaring lion filled the entrance, blotting out the view of the street like a snarling thundercloud.

To give Ariel her due, she caught up pretty fast. What had begun with Jo dragging her ended up with her grabbing Jo and flying backwards, deeper into the ticket hall.

What saved them was that the frozen people were as immovable to the lion as they were to anything else. They acted like speed bumps and traffic bollards, making the great beast slow right down and pick his way through them, his head ducked in below the canopied entrance as he pushed his way in after Jo and Ariel.

Ariel flew them over the ticket barriers and hovered, suddenly indecisive.

'Go down!' said Jo. 'Follow the escalators.'

Two escalators angled downwards right in front of them.

Ariel still hovered. Jo could see her looking for another option.

'What are you waiting for!' she said. 'Move!'

'Looking for another exit!' said Ariel, sounding flustered.

The lion was working its way over the obstacle course of frozen people. Once it got over the ticket barrier it would have a clear enough space to jump at them. It was nearly there.

'Come ON!' said Jo. 'GO!'

Ariel was biting her lip, eyes going left and right.

'Why aren't we moving?' said Jo.

'I've never been underground,' said Ariel.

'Ever been eaten by a lion?' said Jo.

Ariel still wavered. Jo tried to wrench herself free of her grasp.

'Well, I'm going,' she gasped. 'I'm real, right? Not like you. I don't get a reset at midnight if this goes wrong. Let me go!'

Ariel stared at her as if she'd been slapped. Then the lion roared, and she rolled in the air and shot like a bullet straight down the barrel of the escalator tunnel. It was a long way down, and she flew well until they were about halfway. Then she gasped, her body shuddering and sputtering, and Jo felt the power go out of her as they tumbled and hit the divider running down between the up and the down escalators. It was lucky that Ariel hit first, because she was made of metal. The barrier was smooth, shiny steel, which made it an excellent slide, but there were bumps and protuberances on it that were there especially to stop daredevils using it as one. If Jo had been underneath she would have been pretty badly banged up, given the speed at which they hit. As it was, metal slid almost frictionless on metal, which was good from the point of getting away from the lion, but bad from the point at which they ran out of escalator and went sprawling on the hard stone floor of the concourse beyond.

Jo tucked and rolled, and came to a painful stop against a nun's legs. Ariel landed upside down against the end wall, smacking home next to a busker with an accordion, sending his capful of coins spattering across the floor.

'Ouch,' she said.

Jo scrambled to her feet and limped across to her.

'Come on,' she said, casting her eye back up the escalator.

Because of the angle, she couldn't see all the way to

the top, but she could hear some pretty heavy and ominous scraping.

She pulled Ariel to her feet. 'We've got to go,' she said.

Ariel looked at her.

'What?' said Jo.

'I can't fly,' said Ariel, her eyes dull with shock.

'You can't fly?' said Jo.

Ariel shook her head.

'It's gone.' Her eyes brimmed with tears. Her lip actually quivered.

The noise from the escalator turned from scrabbling to slithering, then the unmistakable screech of heavy metal sliding against metal.

'I don't know what to do,' sobbed Ariel. 'I don't know . . .'

Jo slapped her. 'Run!' she said. 'You run!'

And she grabbed her and forced Ariel forwards. The sobbing turned to gasping as the two of them powered along the tunnel towards the platform, dodging in and out of the unmoving commuters, as behind them the huge bronze lion slid downhill like an incoming express train.

They heard it crash to a halt at the bottom but didn't look back as they ran.

They hit the split between the northbound and southbound platforms. There was a train in one, and the other was empty.

'We've got to get back into the air,' said Ariel.

'Only way back up is the way we came. Past the lion,' panted Jo. 'Keep moving!'

She didn't want to go into the tunnels. She really didn't. There was a live electric rail in there that would fry them if they touched it, and that was just the first of a hundred or so reasons. However, they might have to. But then, if they could go into a tunnel, the lion could too, so maybe *that* should be the first reason, because at least right now the lion was a bit hampered by having to negotiate all the frozen people it couldn't push over. In the tunnel it would have a clear run at them.

Jo was doing all this thinking as she ran, trying to make up a plan on the move. Her eyes scanned the signs on the platform. Maybe there was a fire exit. Or a door to a narrow passage the staff used. But there weren't any useful signs, or if there were, they were moving too fast for her to make them out between the blur of garish posters plastered to the walls, posters advertising museums and holidays and books and movies, lots of movies. If this was a movie, she thought bitterly, there'd be a crawl space or something, a convenient access hatch and a behind-the-scenes piece of ducting they could hide in, but this wasn't a movie, and there was nothing convenient about what it was. Which was terrifying, all the more so because the lion scrambled out onto the platform behind them and roared. Jo made the mistake of looking back and meeting its glare over the heads of the static crowd clogging the platform.

It blinked lazily at her and then confirmed all her worst fears by simply avoiding the barrier of people and slipping off the platform down onto the rails, which gave it a clear run at them. It filled the space, its head and mane almost as big as a train as it powered towards them.

Ariel's gaze met hers, and the resigned, dead look in her eyes shocked Jo. She didn't waste breath trying to shout her back to life. She just grabbed her and shoved her back through one of the arches that connected the two platforms.

They stumbled through and found themselves facing the train. The doors were wide open.

Jo pulled Ariel onto the train. It was one of the new ones that had no dividers between the carriages, so that once inside you were on one long tube, as if you had entered the belly of a snake.

They ran towards the end of the snake. If it had been full of people they would have been really safe. The lion could not have squeezed its way after them.

But, along with all the other bad cards Jo had received in the last twenty-four hours, fate had dealt them an empty train. It might be a new day, but her unlucky streak was definitely unbroken.

They felt the train lurch beneath their feet; they spun and looked back.

The lion had forced its great head inside the carriage behind them, and was now carefully tunnelling in, belly low to the ground as it crawled forwards, filling the space as it came. It was an awkward progress, but it did move it inexorably forwards.

Jo turned. They had run out of train. She looked back at the crawling lion and realised with a lift in her heart that it was now so constricted that they could escape it by getting out of the train through the side door, because by the time it had squeezed after them they would be long gone.

She turned to the side, expecting to see the next doorway, and saw the door. Closed. And beyond it no platform to escape to, just the black wall of the tunnel.

'Great,' she spat. 'Of course . . .'

'What?' said Ariel.

'It's a short platform. You can't get out of the front coach.'

She looked round again. There wasn't enough time to get back up the carriage to an open platform door, because the lion would get there first. They might as well save time and just run straight down his throat.

'We're trapped,' said Ariel. Her voice sounded dull and as dry as rust.

18

Going sideways, fast

The roar of the hunting lion had chilled Will's bones. He didn't know for sure that it had been on Jo's trail, but it wasn't a bad bet. He'd just have to trust she had got to a place of safety, because the alternative was too horrible a thought to consider without freezing like a rabbit caught in headlights. In fact, if Will stayed still and thought too hard about things he would find it harder and harder to move when he needed to. So the answer was to keep on moving. He pointed to a half-open window across the alley.

'We don't need to use the streets,' he said. 'We go sideways. We use the buildings as cover.'

And before Wolfie or Tragedy could say anything, he checked that no lion was peering down the alley before he crossed it and boosted himself into the window.

He landed on a desktop between a computer screen and a man frozen in the act of working a keyboard.

'Sorry,' he muttered on reflex, and slid over the man's paperwork and down onto the ground.

Tragedy and Wolfie followed him.

They worked their way through the building until they got to the other side, where they looked through another fire-exit door across the next alley. There was a service door standing wide open in the wall of the adjacent building as a man wheeled in a cask of beer on a dolly.

By hopping alleys and winding their way through the interiors of six different buildings they got themselves a block and a half away from the besieged hotel.

Then they had to cross a main road, and once they had checked it out and decided it was safe, they found themselves in the open again.

'Zis is fun,' grinned Wolfie.

'No, it isn't,' said Will. 'This is Oxford Street.'

He looked both ways down the wide and crowded thoroughfare. It was teeming and huge and hard to check out properly and full of places from which predators' eyes could even now be hungrily scanning for them. The thought of it made his mouth dry.

'It's massive,' he said. 'Anything could be watching us and we wouldn't see it until it was too late.'

'Do we need to cross it then?' said Tragedy. 'I mean, we could carry on with the house-hopping on this side. Seems to work and Wolfie's right – it's sorta fun seeing inside all these houses . . .'

'This is not FUN!' Will said. A little too loudly. All three of them knew this instantly and went very still, listening and looking. Nothing seemed to have heard them.

The idea of having something as silly as 'fun' while his mother was alone and unmoving and vulnerable in the cold street, where any of the malicious statues or dragons could just amble up and hurt her, or while his sister was lost who-knew-where made Will's blood pound with anger. He tried to control it. There wasn't time to explain to them.

'Sorry,' Will whispered between gritted teeth. 'But seriously. This isn't fun. This is life or death. Jo and I swore we wouldn't get split up. But now we have. And we said if that happened, we'd rendezvous at Coram's Fields . . .'

'By your mum,' said Tragedy, remembering.

Coram's Fields was where he had met them, just after the whole world had gone so gut-wrenchingly pear-shaped and jammed to a shuddering stop.

'Yes,' said Will. 'And that's north of here. Round

the back of the museum and on a bit. And this road runs east–west. So we have to cross it.'

Filax showed the way. He crawled across, slow and low to the ground, as if stalking a rabbit. He passed two taxis and slipped round the back of a topless tourist bus, and got to the other side. Slinking between the pedestrians, he bounded into a narrow street. He disappeared from view for a long minute, but then he returned, stood in the entrance to the alley and wagged his tail.

''E's saying it's all clear,' said Tragedy. ''E's a corker of a dog, isn't 'e?'

'He is,' said Will, dropping to all fours. He was already so wet that crawling across the puddled pavement and the rain-slick street were going to make no difference to his general level of comfort.

The three of them beetled across the tarmac, keeping as low to the ground as possible. They had just got to the back of the tourist bus when Filax barked and they all froze in their tracks.

The bark was loud, challenging and definitely an urgent warning.

19

Emergency exit

Jo and Ariel were backed up against the driver's door at the front of the Underground train, dead-ended with nowhere to run. Ariel was tugging at the door as if unable to believe that it wouldn't open. Jo was staring at the head of the lion that filled the carriage as it belly-crawled towards them. It was like being inside a syringe, watching the plunger coming to squash you.

She looked at the window beside her and saw the dirty black tunnel wall beyond it. And she saw the little glass window above.

The one marked 'EMERGENCY ONLY'.

She leapt forwards and elbowed the glass. Ariel spun at the sharp crack and threw her a despairing look.

'What?'

Jo snatched the torch out of the emergency box and pointed at the window.

'Window. Break it.'

Ariel hesitated. Losing her powers had drained her so that her normal sparkiness was almost extinguished and replaced with a leaden dullness.

'It's glass, you're metal. BREAK IT!' snapped Jo. That lion was getting much too close.

Ariel seemed to wake up a bit. She crossed to the window and punched it. Nothing happened.

'Ow!' she said.

Jo realised something had broken inside Ariel – not inside her hand, but inside her head. She'd lost her usual sassy vigour, the cockiness that had made her so annoying, but which had also made her energetic. This reduced Ariel was nothing like the heroic Ariel who had stepped in front of the dragon's blast to save Will. This was a loser Ariel. And right now Jo needed the other one badly, or they weren't going to get out of this.

There was only one way to get her back, and that was to insult her.

'I thought you were great,' Jo sneered. 'I thought you were something.'

She was hoping there was still enough unbroken Ariel within her to catch fire at the dismissive scorn in Jo's voice.

'I thought you were something,' she repeated.

'Not a blubbering nothing.'

Ariel's head came up a fraction. 'I am something,' she said, but her voice was still sluggish.

'You're not,' spat Jo. 'Look at you. Whining and giving up.'

'I'm not,' said Ariel.

'Yes, you are,' said Jo, eyeing the approaching lion. 'You're nothing.'

Ariel glared at her. Was that something kindling in her eyes?

'You're worse than nothing,' said Jo, choosing the next words as if they were the final arrow in her quiver, hoping it was the one that would hit the mark, because if it didn't, any second now the lion would have squirmed so close to them that it would be able to swat them with a paw. 'You're just ordinary.'

The word thunked home. Ariel's eyes ignited.

'ORDINARY?'

She lashed out at the emergency window.

It smithereened into tiny chunks of safety glass, and then she hit it again and the bits dropped away, letting in the faint breeze from the tunnels and the grimy and faintly sulphurous smell that came with it.

'You think that is ordin—' she began.

Jo just grabbed her, scrambled over the seat and

dropped down the outside of the train.

When you're running on adrenalin, time and memory go funny. It's like the fight-or-flight mode needs all the juice in you, so it doesn't bother remembering what you're doing, because that would be a waste of energy, energy needed to power your legs and heart and get you as far away from the danger in as short a time as possible.

Because of this, what happened next was, for Jo, a series of snapshots, not a continuous memory.

The drop to the rails was further than she expected. Her leg hurt.

She looked back towards the platform, a slice of light between the curved train side and the wall of the tunnel.

Only ten feet away.

Something large and dark was on the platform. Moving.

Something small and gold and rat-shaped ran ahead of it and peered down the track at them.

It would have no trouble fitting through the curved slice of space and chasing after them.

She was running.

The golden rat stared down the gap between the train and the tunnel mouth, watching the circle of light made by Jo's torch get smaller and smaller as they sprinted off into the cavernous maw of the Underground.

Behind it on the platform a second huge bronze lion roared in frustration.

Then the rat turned. The other lion, the one that had been crawling up the inside of the train, began to back awkwardly out of the doors. It came bottom first, belly to the ground as it squeezed itself free. It was definitely an undignified exit for something that thought of itself as king of the jungle, and perhaps because of this it did not roar, but just hissed with a sound like a steam-escape valve letting pressure out of a boiler that was about to explode.

The rat scampered away from the tunnel mouth, moving fast. Although it was a metal rat, it had a real rat's habit of keeping to the angle of the wall where possible, so it raced along the edge of the platform further from the rails, and then followed it as it right-angled to an exit. It chicaned round the frozen commuters and leapt up onto the rubber handrail of the escalator. It flowed uphill at speed, jumping over the hands of the unmoving passengers with a series of sinuous lollops that didn't slow its progress at all.

Reaching the level of the street it hurled itself to the

floor and skittered out.

Outside, it slid to a stop, the water on the pavement spraying the bird who was waiting for it.

The rat looked up into the beady stone eye of Horus the hawk, transfixed by the blue radiating from it like a searchlight.

In the museum Bast perched on the edge of the sarcophagus, staring at the surface of the blue light that filled it like a heavy liquid. And at the centre of it she saw what Horus saw, as if the stone hawk was a television camera and the sarcophagus a screen.

The rat chittered at her.

THE TUNNELS, YOU SAY, said the cat.

The rat chittered some more.

NO, said the cat. NOT A JOB FOR LIONS THEN.

GO BACK, said the cat. I WILL GIVE YOU THE ARMY YOU REQUEST. IT IS IN MY POWER. WHAT MAGIC I MAKE, I CAN UNMAKE. I AM BAST.

The rat bobbed in what was almost a curtsey, and doubled back into the Underground station.

On the edge of the sarcophagus Bast reached a paw down and lazily stirred the surface of the light. The view from Horus's eye disappeared and the blue light seemed to bulge upwards towards the cat's face as if it was alive. Alive and hungry.

The cat snarled at it, showing its fangs. The light slapped back and became flat and glassy. The cat leaned over and stared at itself in the now obedient and mirror-smooth surface.

WHAT FLESH MOVES BY FOUR LEGS UNDER THE GROUND I RELEASE FROM THE CURSE OF STILLNESS TO DO MY WILL . . .

20

Wolfie's weapon

The echo of Filax's warning bark was still resonating in the night air as Will rolled sideways so that his back was against the bus.

He looked over at the dog. His first instinct was to shush it. Then he saw the intensity with which Filax was staring at something above him, and he ditched the first instinct and went straight to instinct number two: which was to follow the dog's gaze.

He looked straight upwards. Right into the eyes of a huge bronze lion that had been lying in wait four metres overhead, on the open top of the tourist bus, biding its time.

As it snarled and launched itself, he rolled sideways, hit the sharp edge of the back step and without thought threw himself inside the bus. What saved him were two things. One was not thinking and just reacting. The second that it was an old Routemaster bus, one of the kind that had an open platform on the back corner for getting in and out.

As the lion hit the pavement and Tragedy rolled left and Wolfie leapt right to avoid getting squashed flat, Will hurled himself into the stairwell to the upper floor. The lion was a big one, and now he was momentarily safe he had time for one thought, which was that it would not be able to get inside the narrow space in which he was now hiding.

As the lion regained its balance and spun to spring after Will, Wolfie leapt inside the bus and jammed in with him.

Tragedy didn't move fast enough.

The lion backed him up against a taxi.

Will saw a fragmented view of what happened next through the rain-spattered window of the bus.

Tragedy saw he had nowhere to go. So he grinned as convincingly as he could and reached out a hand.

'Here, kitty kitty,' he said. 'Who's a nice kitty then, eh?'

The lion cocked its head.

'You two get out of here,' said Tragedy out of the side of his mouth, without breaking eye contact with the lion. 'I got kitty here, don't I, nice old soppy moggy that you are, ain'tcha?'

The lion cocked its head on the other side.

For a moment Will thought it was, impossibly, going to be OK.

And then the lion roared, blowing Tragedy's hair back off his forehead with the force of it, and leapt at him.

Filax T-boned the lion in mid-air, ramming into its side like a snarling marble missile. Because the lion was airborne, and the dog had timed his attack to hit it as soon as its paws left the ground, it had no way of resisting the force and direction of the impact. Filax knocked the lion sideways so that it missed Tragedy and hit the traffic light on the pedestrian island in the middle of the road with a loud BONG that both stunned it and bent the metal pole ten degrees off vertical.

Tragedy didn't hang around to see what happened next, because another lion came bounding down the road, closing at speed. Filax saw it and disappeared as Tragedy scrambled onto the bus.

'Up!' he said. 'UP. That little bleeder will get in here easy!'

They tumbled upwards onto the open deck. The sight it gave them of the street was certainly scenic but not at all cheerful. There was movement all around as animal shapes raced towards them from the south and east and west.

'We're not safe up here,' said Will, looking down at the stunned lion, who was trying groggily to get to its feet. 'That one got up here once; it looks like it'll have no problem in repeating the trick . . . and then we're toast.'

Tragedy nodded. 'No worries. We got a secret weapon, remember?'

Will stared at him and the grinning boy in the wig and fooffy shirt.

'Tradge,' he said, feeling the bitter taste of defeat beginning to sour his mouth as he spoke. 'You were brave as hell down there, calling the lion "kitty", but you've got a screw loose if you think a violin's going to stop anything.'

'Not a violin, dummy,' said Wolfie. 'A *wunderkind*!'

And then, as if there was some hidden conductor in the sky watching for his cue, there was a flash of lighting, and a crash of thunder that made Wolfie throw back his head and roar with delighted laughter. He stepped up onto the seats and stood with one leg cocked on the railing of the bus, looking all round him at the approaching animals as he slipped the violin under his chin and began to work his bow across the strings, sending raindrops flying into a fine mist as he played with dizzying speed.

And as he played, Will understood. The secret weapon wasn't Wolfie or the violin: it was his music. It was extraordinary and exciting and moving and familiar and unexpected and magical. It was complicated and it was simple. It was all that and many more contradictory things, but most of all, despite all its spellbinding intricacy, the thought came to Will that it was pure: it was as pure as the clean, cold water from the original well that all the greatest music comes from. He shook his head. That wasn't the kind of thought he normally had, but then this wasn't the kind of music he normally liked; except now he was under a spell, like the animals that had slowed and begun to gather tamely in front of the bus, looking up at the wild boy making the enchanted bow fly across the strings of his violin.

Even the stunned lion looked happy as it came and sat calmly beneath the bus, looking up.

'Wow,' said Will.

'Secret weapon,' said Tragedy.

'How did you know?' said Will.

'Music hath charms to soothe the savage breast,' said Tragedy. 'One of the things Old Black says.'

He nodded at the growing crowd of lions and cats gathering on the south-east corner of the bus, like a

well-ordered audience at an impromptu concert.

'And you don't get more savage breasts than that of a lion, I can tell you that. I nearly widdled myself down there.'

'But you didn't,' said Will. 'You were braver than the lion.'

Tragedy nodded and looked at Will with a face that, despite the rain, for just a short moment shone like the sun. Will realised once more how starved of praise and affection the small statue must be.

Tragedy found his normal face again. He beckoned Will to the back of the bus, away from the southern edge. He looked over the railing to the north. Will was surprised and cheered to see Filax back in the alleyway, wagging his tail at him. Dogs can't speak, but his look was definitely saying, 'Let's GO!'

'While Wolfie's got 'em all calmed up over there, let's scarper,' said Tragedy. 'If we get split up, we'll meet you at Coram's Fields. OK?'

Once more it was time to move, not think. Will nodded. He squeezed Tragedy's shoulder and then slipped over the side of the bus and hung down.

'Hold on,' said Tragedy, and took hold of his wrist, leaning over and lowering him a bit further so the drop would be easier. Their eyes met. Will nodded. Tragedy winked and let him go.

Will hit the ground softly and turned. Tragedy was already after him. Will caught him as he dropped, and put him on his feet. Then they ran as low and as silently as they could to join Filax. Will glanced back for one last quick look at Wolfie, who now bestrode the front of the bus as if it were a ship and he was some wild and elemental figurehead, his arm shuttling back and forwards as the music worked its glamour on the watching beasts.

As Will turned and ran north with Filax and Tragedy he felt like he had to physically tug himself from the magnetic pull of the music step by step. As the distance increased, the pull became easier to escape, but for the first few hundred metres it was only the competing tug drawing him towards his sister that allowed him to move at all.

Will had felt a lot of things in his life. He had felt bad. He had felt guilty. He had felt pain and he had felt fear, huge fear that sucked his mind away and left a howling echo-chamber of dread in its place. He had felt of lot of all those things especially intensely in the time since the world had stopped and trapped him and Jo in this living nightmare. But he had never, ever felt the thing he now felt jarring through him with every step he ran: he felt fractured – dangerously, terrifyingly fractured, like a thin crack was spreading through the very core of him, of what made him Will.

If she was not at Coram's Fields, he didn't know what he would do. But he began to dread that he would break. Break, shatter and go mad. Or worse.

21

Rat run

Jo must have switched on the torch by reflex, because it bounced a ring of light on the soot-blackened tunnel ahead of them as they ran.

Ribbed sections of tube blurred past.

Dark cables of all sizes, thick to thin, accompanied their flight, making looped swags along the tunnel walls like carefully draped intestines.

It was as if they'd escaped into the belly of a much darker and bigger beast than the train.

They ran close to the side of the tunnel, keeping clear of the fourth rail as well as the third electrified rail in the middle and to the side of the two regular ones on which the train's wheels ran. You could see the electrified ones because they were mounted on white china insulating pads.

Jo didn't know if both electric rails would kill you. She thought for some reason it was only the middle one. But she was not going to take any chances.

The gravel and clinker base of the tunnel crunched as they ran, and for a while, after they'd escaped the angry roars of frustration from the lions, who had been unable to squeeze past the train and get into the tunnel behind them, there was no other noise.

As her eyes adjusted to the light, Jo noticed patches of bluish light on the ground ahead and all around them. It was the same frozen light that covered the people and the soldier-statues. She looked more closely at the next patch as she approached it. At first she thought it was a pair of shoes. It was about the same shape and size, but then, as she focused the beam of the torch on it, she realised with a shudder that it was a pair of rats.

She hated rats.

She knew the tube was full of them. She'd once stood close to the edge of a platform and looked down at the grubby floor between the tracks and seen three large black rats scuttling unconcernedly back and forth, just a few short feet from the unsuspecting crowd of commuters above. Her dad had pulled her back. It was the time that he had explained why getting close to the edge was so dangerous, not just because a train might come and squash you, but because of the electric rails. He'd pointed them out to her. She'd asked how the rats didn't get electrocuted; he'd said rats were pretty clever. He'd sounded quite impressed. He said he'd seen a lot of bad places in the world, and that rats always survived.

It had given her nightmares, all those black furry shapes with their long naked tails, scurrying about unseen, just beneath the skin of the city, in the walls and under the floors. That's where her fear of rats had begun. But, on the plus side, that was when she'd got wised up about the lethal rails, so that was good.

She wished her dad was with her now, and thinking of him led her to think of her mum, frozen and alone in the empty city. At least wherever he was he was surrounded by his fellow soldiers. They'd left her mum alone and open to the elements and anything bad that decided to drop out of the sky on her. And that started her thinking of Will, and that didn't help anything. She clenched her jaw and ran on.

'I am not ordinary,' said Ariel eventually, as they rounded a long curve and saw the lights of a distant platform beckoning them.

She sounded out of breath and angry.

'And I do not like running,' she added. 'It is much more tiring than flying.'

'I was just trying to snap you out of it,' said Jo. She

was running lopsidedly, her leg screaming at her to stop and rest. She ignored it. 'You went into a funk.'

'A funk?' said Ariel. 'What is a "funk"?'

'You slowed down. You got frozen in the headlights. You stopped thinking.'

Ariel snorted dismissively. But she didn't have a ready reply. Maybe, like Jo, she needed every bit of breath to keep moving.

They crunched grimly onwards towards the light, which didn't seem to be getting any closer. And then Jo's knee gave way and she gasped and fell, her hand reaching out instinctively, trying to steady herself.

She fell straight towards the electric rail.

Snatching her hand back, she tried to corkscrew out of the way, but with only one leg it was hopeless. Her eyes screwed shut on reflex and then her arm was wrenched out of its socket and she stopped moving.

She opened her eyes. And saw the electric rail an inch from her nose.

Ariel pulled her slowly backwards, away from the danger.

'That was close . . .' Jo gasped. 'Much too close. Thank you . . .'

Ariel smiled. 'It wasn't just close,' she said. 'It was extraordinary. The speed of my reflexes? Extraordinary

'. . . rather like me, no?'

The old Ariel was back. Conceited. Vain. Boastful.

Jo was surprised to find she had missed her. Then Ariel did a remarkable thing. She smiled and punched Jo on the arm.

'I'm joking, fool.'

'What?' said Jo.

'I'm saying thank you for snapping me out of it back there.'

This was new. Ariel sounded almost . . . normal.

'I don't work properly down here. You saw me crash-land on the escalator.'

'I felt it,' said Jo. 'Remember?'

Ariel smiled grimly.

'Well, I've never not worked before. I've always been able to fly. But I think that because I was made as a spirit of the air, I don't work if I go back into the ground.'

'I'm made of metal,' she added in explanation. 'Where does metal come from?'

'Underground,' said Jo. 'OK. I get it.'

'And me not being able to fly. Well, that's like you not being able to walk,' said Ariel. 'You can't imagine how that feels.'

'Actually I can,' said Jo. And without thinking

why she was doing it she stopped, bent down and hiked up the leg of her jeans, shining the torch on the scars. 'I couldn't walk for quite a while. That's why I run funny.'

Ariel peered at her knee. She opened her mouth to say something, and then her eyes shifted.

'Jo,' she said, and even as Jo got a small prick of pleasure from the fact that she had used her name for the first time, she got a bigger stab of alarm from the look that suddenly washed over Ariel's face.

'What?' she said.

'Look,' said Ariel. 'The lights are going out.'

For a moment Jo did not see what she meant. The lights on the distant platform were strong as ever. Her torch was unwavering. And then she saw what Ariel was referring to.

The small blurs of rat-shaped blue light scattered between them and the platform were blinking out, one after another, as if a wave of darkness was sweeping along towards them at track level.

'Why's that happening?' said Jo. 'Those are rats. Something's snuffing out the rats.'

'No,' said Ariel. 'No . . . I don't think anything's snuffing them out . . .'

And as the lights went out, there was a small but

growing noise of tiny claws scrabbling on concrete.

'I think they're coming back to life.'

'You think the city's coming back to life?' said Jo, her heart beginning to soar in relief.

Ariel pointed at the blue human shapes on the platform.

'No,' she said, beginning to back up. 'I don't think the city's coming back to life. I think the rats are coming back for us. Run!'

22

Herded

Music may be magic but it fades with distance, and the further Will ran with Tragedy and Filax, the more he was aware that they were leaving the zone of safety that Wolfie was radiating from his violin.

Because of this he slowed again and began checking side streets before he crossed them, and it was thanks to this caution returning just in time that he caught sight of the two cheetahs.

Lions are one thing. Cheetahs, even bronze ones, are both lighter and somehow more immediately dangerous. A bit like the difference between a sharp arrow and a spear: the spear has more weight and heft, but if you had to choose between the two being pointed at you in anger, you have the nasty suspicion that an arrow will move much, much faster. Not that these cheetahs were, at the moment, moving very fast at all . . .

Nor were the cheetahs actually stalking them. In

fact, the first time Will caught sight of them, they didn't seem to have seen him at all. They were on a parallel road, also heading north, and as they padded over the cross street he happened to look east and see them. He instantly went very still, as did Filax and Tragedy. The cheetahs just ghosted on northwards and disappeared from view.

'That was close,' breathed Tragedy, and they jogged on for a couple of streets east to put some space between them and the two predators. It took them away from the direction Will wanted to go in, but sometimes he remembered his dad saying that the longest way is the shortest, because it gets you there, whereas short cuts can be dangerous. It hadn't made much sense to him when his dad said it when they were out on a dog walk, but now he realised his dad must have been repeating something he'd learned in the army. There was no point taking the straightest path to Coram's Fields if it walked them straight down the gullet of two very rangy-looking predators. More haste, less speed was another way his dad had of saying it. Thinking of his dad gave him the familiar ache; if only he was able to talk to either of his parents about all this. If only they were there with him. Having to do it all on his own, or all on his and Jo's own, was horrible.

He'd spent a lot of his life in a hurry to be grown up, and right now he'd much rather a grown-up would show up and make some sense of this nightmare he was trapped in.

Either there were four cheetahs, or the ones to the west of them were fast movers when they were out of sight, because it seemed only a couple of minutes before Tragedy held up a hand and stopped. Without moving his head, Will swivelled his eyes left, and sure enough, there were two very similar cheetahs standing in the cross street to their east. He had a sense that this time the cats saw them as they stood there, tails swishing back and forth in lordly disdain. He flinched as they stepped forwards, anticipating them blurring into a fast, running attack that would eat up the hundred metres that separated them. He knew cheetahs were the fastest animals on Earth, but in this case they neither sprinted nor moved towards them. Instead they just padded away, out of sight, this time heading south, away from them.

'They must have seen us,' said Will.

'Yeah,' said Tragedy. 'I don't like it.'

Filax growled.

'Neither does he,' said Will.

* * *

The next time they saw the cheetahs they were ahead of them, which forced them to go east a bit, until the animals appeared to their east again and sent them north. And the more Will caught glimpses of the cats, the more he felt there was something wrong, something deeper beneath the obvious fact that the cats were controlling them. He couldn't quite put his finger on it, and he felt stupid because of it. Fear and exhaustion were beginning to fuggle his mind. He could certainly put his hand on that.

'I don't think they're hunting us,' said Will, though that wasn't the thing.

'No,' agreed Tragedy. 'I think they're doing what cats do with mice. I think the bleedin' things are playing with us, 'cos they definitely see us. I seen 'em looking out of the side of their eyes, pretending not to look.'

'I think we're being herded,' said Will slowly. 'I think they're acting like sheepdogs.'

'So what do we do?' said Tragedy.

'We don't act like sheep,' said Will, surprised at the grimness in his voice.

The next time the cheetahs appeared it was to their right, obviously intending to send them east again. Instead of doing that, Will waited until they had strolled out of view and then led Tragedy and Filax at a silent run straight towards the very intersection the cheetahs had just vacated. They paused to check the way was clear, and then ran on through it and sped up.

'Come on,' said Will. 'Got to make up for lost time. We've been pushed too far east.'

They zigged and zagged west and north, from intersection to intersection, beginning to believe they had shaken off the cheetahs, right until the moment they came to a wide street of at least six lanes, which had the unwelcome bonus feature of two waiting cheetahs in the middle of it.

And then the herding began in earnest.

Whether the cheetahs were angry or just stepping up the tempo of the game, things began to happen quickly. There was no doubt that the cats saw them, because they snarled and ran at them.

And though they could clearly have leapt and attacked at any moment, they didn't. Instead, just like the sheepdogs that Will had likened them to, they curved and ran round them, growling and snapping at their heels, so wherever they tried to escape to, there was always one or other of the animals there to intercept and push them back on course. And there was no doubt about it, there was a definite course and the cheetahs were absolutely pushing them towards something. The trouble with this – one of the many troubles with this, of course – was that once they were running scared (and Will was perfectly clear about the fact his legs were now being fuelled by pure high-octane terror) it was impossible to think straight or work out how to escape from the pell-mell rush towards their doom.

Filax did manage to turn and try and attack one of the cheetahs but the cat just swatted him away and jumped nimbly right over him, so that the dog found itself running rather ignominiously behind the main group, trying to catch up. Clearly the cats had little time for him and were concentrating on Will.

'I think they just want me,' he panted, looking sideways at Tragedy. 'You should stop . . .'

'I ain't stopping for no one!' gasped Tragedy. 'They got big curved teeth on them like dirty great Arab daggers, in case you ain't noticed.'

Will had noticed. It was hard not to, because of the snarling and panting as the cats chivvied them along the road. There was definitely something about the cheetahs that he should be able to put his finger on, but still he couldn't.

He knew there was going to be something bad

at the end of this run, and whatever it was, as exhaustion began to make him stumble instead of run smoothly, he hoped it would either give him a chance to talk, or be very quick. He was disoriented and wondered if he was being run straight towards the museum and the horrible cat. Well, that might be good. He might be able to plead, or explain. Not that he knew what he was going to explain, but talking . . .

Talking turned out not to be an option.

The cheetahs bounded in front of him, making him twist and career down a narrow mews passage. He was so busy keeping his balance that he didn't realise he was about to crash headlong into the waiting gorilla until he hit it.

He bounced off the unmoving block of living bronze and sprawled, winded, at its feet. He looked up in horror.

The gorilla was massive above him, blocking out the night sky, a looming cliff of bunched muscle with a mouthful of seriously lethal teeth that made the cheetahs' fangs look puny by comparison.

Will was stunned by the impact, but he could see that even more frightening was the fact that the gorilla had a second head sticking out of one of its shoulders, smaller than the massive main head, a more delicate human head with a waving topknot of hair on it. It was like something from a mutant horror film.

He was about to shout, or maybe scream, or maybe just roll into a ball and pretend none of what was about to happen was real, when he saw Tragedy leap over him and hurl himself at the mountainous primate.

He couldn't believe his eyes, couldn't think what Tragedy was hoping to achieve by this suicidal head-on assault.

And he certainly couldn't understand the exultant whoop of pleasure Tragedy gave as he slammed into the gorilla and let it hoist him up into the air like a baby.

'Put me down, you big old banana-breath!' he chuckled, clearly not minding a bit.

As the gorilla held him up Will saw that it was not some freakish two-headed monster statue, but a terrifyingly huge but perfectly common or garden gorilla with a small bronze girl riding piggyback on it.

'Put him down, Guy,' said the girl. Her voice had a mild Indian accent that lilted gently and made her seem on the bubbling point of laughter.

'Will,' said Tragedy as the gorilla lowered him to the ground. 'Will, this is AP, my mate. We call her 'Appy though, cos she always is.'

The girl slid off the back of the gorilla and grinned

at Will. A bronze dove fluttered in from the shadows and sat on her shoulder.

'Hello,' she said, extending her hand rather formally. 'I'm Happy.'

'I know who you are,' said Will, amazed. This was a statue he knew. She was from London Zoo. He'd been there three times. She was normally by a water fountain, reaching up for the dove. She was wearing a high-necked dress, but was barefoot, as if enjoying herself at a children's party. 'You're from the Zoo.'

He shook her hand, which was warm and soft. She had a good firm handshake for a young kid, he thought, and she smiled right into your eyes without a smidgen of shyness. You couldn't help but like her.

'We all are,' she said. 'Me, Guy, the cats.'

He turned to see the two cheetahs were sitting calmly behind him, licking their paws as if they hadn't a shred of interest in him. Filax stood between them, looking confused. Happy walked over and stroked him.

'Hello, dog,' she said. 'I don't know you yet.'

She scratched behind his ears and his tail gave a couple of tentative wags.

'He's Filax,' said Tragedy. 'Brave old hound, he is. Saved my bacon.'

'I can see that,' she said, looking into the dog's eyes. 'I can see he's a brave one. You're a beauty, and you're among friends here.'

Filax's tail lashed the ground and he sat happily between the two cats, as if he understood exactly what she had said to him. Only when he looked at the three statues lined up next to each other did Will see the niggling thing he had been missing about the cheetahs. He looked at Guy the Gorilla, and saw it too. Or rather, he didn't see it in any of them.

'Their eyes,' he said. 'They're not shining with blue light like the other animal statues.'

'No,' said Happy, leaning back against the comforting bulk of the gorilla.

The rain had stopped, and now the main sound of the city was quiet, mixed with dripping gutters and burbling drains.

'The others have had a bad spell put on them. Or a curse.'

'But not these ones?' said Will.

Now he was – gloriously and unexpectedly – NOT about to be killed, he was back to wanting to understand everything.

'No,' she said. 'I think they felt the spell too. But a spell? Or even a curse?' She laughed and shrugged her shoulders. 'That's just magic.'

Will looked back out into the street, seeing all the blue-lit figures of frozen people dripping rainwater onto the pavement.

'Well, "just magic" is doing a pretty good job of messing things up around here, I'd say. It seems it's pretty strong stuff.'

'I know,' she said. 'You're right. But it's not as strong as what binds us together. Me to them. Them to me . . .'

'You have stronger magic?' he said.

She laughed again and shook her head. 'No. We have love. Love is the one thing stronger than anything. Love defeats everything in the end.'

'The animals love her,' said Tragedy. 'Always have.'

'And I love them,' she said.

'But . . .' began Will.

She closed him down with a smile.

'I can't explain it. It's just how I am. How I was made. I'm lucky! I was made with love, to show love.'

'And she's right, Will,' said Tragedy. 'Nothing all girly and weak about love when you look at it like that, is there?'

Will looked at the gorilla and the way it stood protectively around the small girl. Immovable. Like a rock. He nodded. He got it. This was strength.

'I sent the cats out to keep you away from the others,' said Happy, looking at Tragedy. 'Ariel flew by and told us what was happening, just before all the other animals went funny and started drifting towards the museum.'

'Thanks,' grinned Tragedy. 'You nearly killed us with your kindness though, cos we was about to have bleedin' 'eart attacks with all that running.'

'Thank you,' said Will. 'Can you help us get to Coram's Fields?'

'Of course,' said Happy a bit hesitantly. 'But why?'

'Because there's something else there that might be stronger than all this blue magic too,' said Will.

'But maybe you should stay with us. It's safe,' she said. 'No one would attack Guy or anyone he was protecting. Not even a lion.'

'I can't,' he said. 'My sister's there.'

'Sister?' she said.

He nodded. 'Yep. At least I hope she is.'

'You have a sister?' she said.

'Yes,' he said. 'And we swore we wouldn't get split up again, but we did. And my mum too, though she's frozen.'

'Family,' she said, suddenly looking both serious

beyond her years, and, as a result, exactly six years old.

'Yes,' he said.

'Family is important.'

'I know,' he said.

'Family is love too,' she said. 'Guy will go with you to protect you all. If that's OK?'

He grinned back at her.

'It's better than OK. It's brilliant.'

He was grinning because now he knew they had a chance . . .

23

The black tide

Jo and Ariel had no chance.

Jo knew this with the certainty of the freshly doomed. They were deep below the city, running through a network of tunnels with a torch that was beginning to dim and sputter, and the darkness around them was full of not just more darkness but a wakening tide of black-coated rats, rats that were audibly on the move.

They could hear the scrabbling of claws and the rising chitter of the approaching wave of rodents behind them.

'I hate rats,' gasped Ariel. 'I see them at night when they come out on the street.'

'I hate them too,' panted Jo.

'Perhaps they're just panicked,' said Ariel. 'Maybe if we get out of their way they'll just run past us and leave us alone.'

Jo risked a fast look backwards.

She really wished she hadn't. The approaching tide had eyes. In fact, all she could really see were eyes. It wasn't hard, because the eyes were all blazing a horribly familiar frosty blue.

'No,' she panted through gritted teeth. 'Not going to leave us alone. Hunting us.'

There had been a lot of eyes, enough so that the snatched look had left her with the horrible image of a rippling wave of blue lights flowing after them like floodwater down a sewer pipe.

Drowning was a nasty enough thought when it was in water. Drowning in rats was a whole deeper level of horrible nightmarishness.

The torch was definitely losing power. The bobbling halo it cast round them as they sprinted down the ribbed tunnel was getting dimmer with every step.

'This is bad!' puffed Ariel. 'Running is bad. Rats are bad. The dark is bad . . .'

Jo wanted to say wasting your breath is bad too, but she didn't. She had too much of a stitch and needed every cubic centimetre of air her lungs could suck in just to keep her legs pounding along the unforgiving rail-bed.

The tunnel made an endless curve. It straightened out with no welcoming rectangle of a station in view, and then arched in the other direction, making another blind curve that seemed to have no end.

Jo grimaced and risked another fast look back.

The wave of blue eyes had very nearly caught up with them. It was close enough for the backwash of light from her torch to pick out the undulating black fur of the running rats as well as the blue eyes. Filling in the detail of the wave made it worse.

'Come ON!' she gasped at Ariel. 'Faster!'

'I can't!' Ariel gasped. 'I just wasn't made to run . . .'

Jo grabbed her arm and shoved her forwards.

'You weren't made to give up either,' she choked. 'RUN!'

There were lights ahead. For a moment Jo thought they might have a chance of escape if only they could keep on running before they burst or collapsed. But then she saw they were not the welcoming white lights of a platform. These were halogen work lights, and they were aimed at a section of yellow scaffolding tower that stood in the middle of the tracks like a roadblock. Hard-hatted workmen in high-vis yellow jackets were grouped around a supervisor who was pointing at something on a blueprint taped to the wall with a hand that also held a big ring of keys like a janitor would carry.

Jo thought if her heart sank any further it would need its own diving bell: there was no station platform visible beyond the scaffolding tower that they could possibly reach before the rat-tide at their heels engulfed them. And then she saw that the scaffolding extended further than the arched roof of the tube tunnel.

It was an air shaft. And air shafts went upwards.

Just as she saw that, a rat jumped and clawed onto the back of her shoe. She dug in and ran faster, fired by the anticipated nip of a rat bite on her Achilles tendon, but the bite never came as the rat was jarred off by the pounding of her feet.

She saw the ladder on the side of the scaffolding and leapt for it. Ariel was right behind her. They clawed upwards as fast as they could, panting and gasping with the effort, and then they allowed themselves to look down.

The wave of blazing blue-eyed rats surged past the foot of the scaffolding, propelled by an unstoppable forward momentum. The frozen workmen stood unmoving like rocks in a stream as the tide parted on either side of them. At the foot of the ladder there was a bobbling disturbance in the rat river, a kind of rodent eddy as the ones who had been at the

196

forefront of the wave attempted to stop, maintain their footing against the unstoppable tide and get up the ladder after Jo and Ariel. The mass of rats behind them had not seen where their prey had gone, and only this hard core of front runners were attempting to follow them upwards. Luckily the ladder was metal and so gave them poor grip, and the pressure of the rat torrent pounding past them dragged them away.

Ariel and Jo exchanged a grin.

'Close . . .' was all Jo managed to say before going back to the serious business of sucking oxygen into her starved lungs.

After at least a minute of recovery, Ariel nodded. 'Too close,' she managed.

Jo could feel a breeze. It was cool and welcome, and coming from above, and when she looked she saw strips of daylight, where the air shaft ended above ground in a series of louvred grilles. She jerked upwards with her thumb.

'Out,' she said.

'You bet,' said Ariel, and they swarmed up the ladder, heading for the light.

Hope gave them second wind, and they got to the top quickly. The air shaft emerged into a rectangular tower with metal louvres that overlooked a rain-drenched section of the Euston Road. It was jammed with unmoving traffic and frozen people, and in the grey light of dawn it was colourless and lifeless and utterly without any redeeming beauty.

Jo stared at it through the metal strips and thought she had never seen anything so wonderful in her whole life.

'There's a door,' said Ariel behind her.

'Good,' she said, enjoying the sharp wetness of the breeze on her face.

'No,' said Ariel. 'It's locked.'

It was. Definitely, immovably and extraordinarily frustratingly locked solid. And it was metal. And unbreakable.

'Seriously?' Jo asked the universe. The universe didn't reply. Nor did it open the door.

'Jo,' said Ariel. She pointed down.

Jo followed the direction of her finger.

The tide of rats had stopped. Unfortunately it had not gone. It had just stopped moving. And in place of the flow there were hundreds of tiny blue eyes blinking back up at them. It was like looking down on a crowded starscape, and in any other circumstances might even have been a bit pretty. Jo didn't see it like that. She felt the weight of the rat that had attached itself briefly to her leg, and then multiplied it by the number of pairs of eyes staring at her, and that imagined weight terrified her so much it made her want to be sick. Just thinking about falling into that horde made her whole skin itch on the inside, from the nape of her neck to the bottoms of her feet.

'There are keys down there,' she said, wishing she hadn't noticed them. 'The man pointing at the plan had a big ring of them in his hand.'

Ariel tested her weight on a length of safety harness that had been clipped to the top of the scaffolding, and used it to lean far back out over the central void of the shaft. She squinted down.

'I can see it,' she said. 'Lots of keys.'

'Maybe . . .' began Jo.

'I know,' said Ariel. 'But we'd have to go back down there. With them.'

'Maybe they'll get bored and go away,' said Jo hopefully.

'Rats don't get bored,' said Ariel. 'I watch them. They're very tenacious. And resourceful. In fact, they're good at everything, except giving up.'

The sea of waiting eyes looked back up at them, as if to confirm this.

It was a dilemma. The keys were there. The door

meant freedom. But getting the keys meant going down among the bewitched rat army. And – as Jo's dad would say – there was no way that would end up with everyone going home for tea and medals.

Jo thought about it. One of them would have to go. Then she thought some more.

'Ariel,' she said. 'Let go of that safety strap.'

'Why?' said Ariel. 'I'll fall.'

'No, you won't,' said Jo. 'You're above ground now, aren't you?'

Ariel's smile was like a slow sunrise.

She opened her hands and did not fall. Instead she drifted back into the centre of the shaft. She giggled and twirled a bit.

'I am,' she laughed. 'I am myself again! A spirit of air and grace and beauty.'

'Yeah, well, hold on for a minute and stay focused,' said Jo. 'Because we're going to have to work out how low you can go before the flying gets to be a problem again.'

'Why?' said Ariel.

'Because I have a plan. And it really needs you not to drop me,' said Jo. 'Do you think you can stay focused?'

Ariel's laughter pealed round the air shaft.

'I can do anything!' she said, suddenly her old theatrical self again. 'I am Ariel!

'I come
To answer thy best pleasure; be't to fly,
To swim, to dive into the fire, to ride
on the curl'd clouds—'

'Yeah,' interrupted Jo. 'Calm down. We don't need any fire-diving or cloud-riding. I really just need you not to let go of the strap.'

Ariel got serious again as she lowered herself down the shaft to the point where her ability to fly stopped. Jo then joined her with the safety strap and lowered it to make sure it reached from that point to the supervisor. As the strap got close to the bottom, the rats took an interest and the bolder among them hurled themselves up at it. One even got a claw-hold for an instant before Jo cracked the strap like a whip and sent it tumbling back down into the chittering mass below.

'OK,' said Jo. 'When I shout "Up", get me out of there fast, because I don't want to be taking on any passengers.'

The thought of hanging on the end of the strap festooned with angry rats really increased the itchiness under her skin.

Ariel watched her attach the safety harness and the strap, and then wound the outer end of the strap tightly round her wrists and nodded at Jo.

'Good luck,' she said. 'Rather you than me.'

'Trust me,' grimaced Jo. 'If I could fly I wouldn't be the one on this end of the string.'

Ariel let her climb down the ladder until the strap was taut, and then she flew out into the centre of the shaft.

'Hold on!' shouted Jo as she let go and found herself swinging like a wild pendulum.

'Get yourself steady,' Ariel yelled back.

All Jo could see was streaks of hungry blue eyes whipping back and forth beneath her. She managed to slow her swings by grabbing onto the passing scaffolding and braking herself, and then she nodded.

'OK,' she said. 'Lower me.'

Ariel carefully manoeuvred her closer and closer to the supervisor and his pointing hand. Jo put out her own hand and balanced herself against his hard hat, but she was still swinging with enough momentum to knock it off instead. She tried again and grabbed hold of his hair instead.

'Sorry,' she said.

The tumbling hat alerted the rats to her target. And

as Ariel had said, rats are tenacious and resourceful and not a bit stupid. They catch on fast.

By the time Jo had got her hands on the key ring and was beginning to twist it out of his hand, they had not only caught on but had started to use the supervisor's body as a ladder to get to Jo.

By the time she had managed to twist the key ring free, they had reached his waist.

By the time she shouted 'UP', the lead rat had swarmed onto his shoulder.

And by the time Jo felt the strap begin to pull her skywards it was too late. The rat had launched itself high into the air, straight at her face.

Jo's world seemed to go into slow motion at the incoming horror of it all.

She saw the rat's open mouth, the long yellow teeth and the pink gaping maw beyond.

She wrenched her head back on reflex.

The rat's eyes came into view, angry blue and blazing.

Its claws reached for her face.

Impact was unavoidable. But not, she realised in a strange timeless flash of a microsecond, uncontrollable.

She snapped her neck forwards and nutted the rat, dead centre on her forehead.

The perfect headbutt.

It didn't hurt her a bit, but the rat dropped like a stone as Ariel pulled her swiftly in the other direction.

It was like being yanked home by a skyhook, and nothing had felt so good for days.

'Good job,' said Ariel as she watched Jo try the keys until she found the right one, and the door opened on the morning light beyond.

'Just a matter of trying them until I found the right one,' said Jo, breathing in the clean air and stepping out into the light.

'Not that. Nutting the rat,' said Ariel. 'At least, I think it's called nutting. I'm sure I've heard Little Tragedy use the word. Anyway, no one could possibly have done it better. Or more gracefully. Not even me.'

'Thanks,' said Jo. 'From you that's real praise.'

'I know,' said Ariel. Airily. Then she grinned. 'Shall we go to Coram's Fields?' She held out a hand.

'Thought you'd never ask,' said Jo, allowing Ariel to wrap a golden arm round her and lift her into the air. And as they lofted up and over the rooftops of the city she allowed herself the luxury of believing that not only would Will be there waiting, but that they might get the third scarab and revive their mother, and then – for the first time – have a new card to put down in the strange game that the Mighty Bast was playing with the city.

24

Last chance

Will and Jo's mum was going to be exactly where they'd had to leave her, at Coram's Fields, just across the railings from the giant bobbly-trunked trees that overhung the street, frozen in place like all the other people in the city. She would be there, and the third scarab bead would be with her, tucked into her wallet where Will had left it before they had realised the scarabs were a protection against Bast's magic. He looked down at the one on his wrist as they jogged through the street in the pale light of the early morning, Tragedy on one side, Filax behind him, the two cheetahs scouting ahead and, perhaps best of all, the reassuring mass of the huge gorilla rumbling along on his other side.

He knew they were getting close. They were running through one of those split-personality London streets, with an older cream-coloured terrace of Georgian buildings running up one side, facing a long bastion of modernist flats that were stepped back from the street in ascending tiers, like a ziggurat. The neon sign for a cinema still glowed halfway along the concrete structure, and he recognised it as the Brunswick Centre. It was not far from here to Coram's Fields. He picked up the pace.

There was a gaggle of about eight house cats standing on a corner ahead of them, but one hiss from the cheetahs sent them streaking away in all directions, leaping under cars and over walls. It was like being in a running motorcade with the cheetahs as outriders clearing their path. He momentarily wondered what would happen if the cheetahs came face to face with the bigger cats of the London Pride, but then they turned the corner, and there they were.

Coram's Fields. He saw the trees and the railings and the blue glowing frozen people. He recognised their car in its parking space with a jolt of happy recognition, and then he looked across the street to where they had left their mother and saw the space where she should have been. He stumbled and looked wildly around.

She was gone.

He stopped and rested his hands on his knees and suddenly felt the ache of all the running in his legs and lungs. And under that he felt a much worse pain in his heart, because there was an answering void in there that matched the empty space on the street.

'She's gone,' said Tragedy. 'Your mum. She's done a bunk!' He sounded shocked. 'How did that happen then?'

Will stumbled across to the place in the street where by every law of fairness and decency his mother should have been. It wasn't quite a void. There was something there.

There was a funny-shaped slab of plywood, with a stick running up the back, and beside it was a shoe.

He knew the shoe.

He knew the foot that normally filled it.

It was his mother's.

'Oh,' said Tragedy.

'She wouldn't have done a bunk without one of her shoes,' said Will, his voice thick and hesitant, as if saying the obvious conjured the truth of it into being. 'Something took her.'

Tragedy picked up the plywood. It spun in his hands.

'Who took her, I wonder?' he said.

Will looked at the front of the plywood. It was shield-shaped. He read the neon writing.

'GOLF SALE LAST CHANCE!!!'

'No idea,' he said.

'A dragon,' said Jo.

Will's head snapped up and for a moment everything was all right, because there was his sister, gently and silently dropping out of the sky, carried by Ariel, who was, he was delighted to see, whole again.

'Where—' he began, and then she landed and they were hugging and words weren't necessary, or even possible because the hug was a really fierce and tight one. Then he felt her go stiff and push him back. He looked into her face. It was grim and looking at the shield and the void that had contained, that *should* have contained, their mother.

'How d'you know it was a dragon?' he said.

'Because I saw one using that stupid sign like a shield.' She looked at the dragon's shield looped over his shoulder. 'It didn't have one of its own.'

'Oh,' he said, unlooping the shield and looking at it. '*That* dragon . . .'

And before he could finish the sentence, 'that' dragon turned into 'the' dragon, the one that had been hiding in the trees waiting for them, the one that was perhaps too provoked by the sight of the boy hefting his own shield as if it belonged to him to stay still.

The dragon attacked. He burst out of the leaf canopy and swooped at Will and Jo.

If Will had not just taken the shield off his shoulder they would have been toast – literally. The dragon shrieked a twisting rope of blazing wildfire at them, but Will got it up just in time. Flame splashed and lapped round the shield, as if the flickering fingers of fire had a mind of their own and were trying to get a grip on it and wrench it from his grasp.

There was a brief relaxation of pressure as the dragon took a breath, and then he charged forwards, stubby arms and scimitar-like talons reaching for his prize as he ran in down the jet of fire.

'Will!' cried Jo as a tendril of flame caught the bottom of her jeans and lit them.

He reached down with his free hand and smacked the flame out, burning his hand.

Her face looked at his, nose to nose behind the shield wall.

'I can't—' she began.

The cheetahs blurred past her and bowled the dragon's legs out from under him by their sheer velocity. He face-planted and the fire-stream choked off with a heavy and undignified clunk.

He wrenched himself to his feet and took a huge,

whooping inhale of breath. This was going to be the fireblast to end it all.

Guy the Gorilla leapt clean over Will, Jo and the shield, and landed with a ground-shaking thump like a two-ton anvil dropping out of the sky, right in front of the shocked dragon as he opened his mouth to spit fire . . .

The gorilla reached up with one massive hand and clamped the dragon's mouth tight shut.

The dragon scrabbled at the immovable primate with his short front talons while Guy held him at safely at arm's length. Way out of the dragon's reach.

Will and Jo peered out from behind the shield and saw the fire-crop in the dragon's chest beginning to glow redder and redder and then to pale as it reached white heat.

The dragon clearly had no safety valve. His expression became wildly distressed as he tried to escape the muzzle the gorilla had effectively clamped over his jaws.

'Uh-oh,' said Tragedy, coming to stand next to them. He was grinning.

The dragon thrashed frantically.

Guy was immovable.

The dragon's blazing blue eyes pulsed and then he crossed.

And then he went, 'Ulp.'

And then he went very, very still. His eyes now looked panicked and more than a little sickly.

'What?' said Jo, looking at Tragedy, who was now sniggering with glee. He nudged Ariel, who was also smiling.

'What?' said Will.

'He swallowed his wildfire,' said Ariel.

'What does that mean?' said Jo.

Guy let the dragon go. He staggered back and held his belly. His ears were flat to his head. He cowered. They could hear the rumbling from inside his guts. Like a locomotive boiler about to blow.

'Er . . .' said Ariel.

'Put it this way,' said Tragedy. 'Probably best not to stand behind it for a while . . .'

The resultant blast not only took out a generous and entirely innocent section of park hedge, incinerating it, but also seemed to take the fight out of the dragon. He yowled and hopped and tried to pat out the lingering smoulder coming from his bottom, and then he saw a deep puddle and plopped himself down in it. Steam hissed up and obscured the creature for a second and when it cleared, the dragon's face was slack and dopey with happy relief.

Guy knuckled over and stood in front of it again, leaning ominously on his hands. The dragon's ears remained back and submissive. He even managed a sickly attempt at an ingratiating grin.

'Don't see that every day,' said Will.

Jo was looking at something in the gutter.

'Mum's wallet,' she said, scooting forwards and picking it up. She opened it and handed him the scarab on the key ring.

She nodded at the dragon cooling his backside in the puddle.

'Want to try your theory?'

Will didn't need a second invitation. He walked past Guy and steeled himself to touch the dragon. His blue eyes looked at Will in consternation, and he raised a claw as if to ward him off. As if he, the boy, was the stronger one.

Guy growled. The dragon didn't move any more.

Will put the looped key ring carefully over the dragon's talon.

He shuddered. And blinked. And sneezed. And scrunched his eyes shut. And when his eyes opened they were red.

Normal for dragons.

Not blue.

He looked puzzled.

'Guy,' said Will. 'If it moves, punch it, please.'

This was the scariest bit. The scarab kept you safe from Bast's spells. For humans, as he knew from painful experience, it only worked while you were wearing it. He wanted to see if it worked the same way for the statues. Or if it lifted the curse. After all, the magic that froze people was different to the magic that enslaved the statues. Maybe the rules were different.

He removed the scarab and stepped back.

The dragon blinked.

His eyes stayed red.

'Jo,' said Will. 'We just got a break.'

'We just lost our mum,' she replied. She was holding the shoe and the wallet.

'I know,' he said. 'But like Soho Sal said, the universe likes to even things out. So we got a break too.'

He looked at Ariel. 'Can you speak to it?'

She nodded.

'Ask if it took our mother.'

The dragon nodded.

'Where?'

The dragon coughed something at Ariel.

'The museum,' she said.

Will nodded slowly. Then he raised his head and stared into the dragon's eyes.

The dragon coughed and rasped some more.

'He's sorry,' said Ariel.

'That's because he's frightened of the gorilla,' said Jo. 'I don't trust him.'

'Quite right,' said Ariel. 'Never trust a taint. But that's not why he's sorry. He's sorry because when he took your mother to Bast he saw something. Something that frightened him more than Guy or the cheetahs or anything we could do to him. He saw Bast had imprisoned the Temple Bar dragon in a dome of its own fire.'

Tragedy gasped.

'Them silver dragons like him. See, to them the Temple Bar Dragon's special, like your mum or your dad is to you.'

The dragon rasped some more.

'He says Bast is truly, terrifyingly mighty to be able to do this. He says she has an army of animal statues that no one can fight.'

Will stared into the dragon's eyes again, trying to find the core intelligence, trying to make a connection.

'If you help us, I will give you your shield back,' he said.

The dragon croaked.

'He says, do you mean you'll exchange your mother for the shield?' said Ariel.

'No,' said Will. 'I mean, yes, of course I'd like to, but I don't think that'd solve the bigger problem. And I think that's what we've got to do.'

Tragedy looked uncomfortable.

'But you 'eard the scaly bugger here. Bast's got an army! What have we got?'

Will looked at Jo. She nodded and came to stand next to him.

'We've got us,' she said, pointing at Tragedy, and Ariel, and the mountainous gorilla, and the two cheetahs sitting calmly next to Filax. 'We're the Resistance.'

'A guerrilla force,' said Will, looking at Guy. 'No offence.'

Guy grunted, his face as unreadable as ever.

'Bast might have a big army of slaves, but size isn't everything. Nor's fighting. You know what slaves are really bad at?'

There was silence.

'Crosswords?' said Tragedy.

'Shut up,' said Ariel. 'She's being serious.'

'Thinking,' said Will. 'Thinking for themselves. Slaves are good at obeying but bad at thinking. So we're not going to beat them by fighting. We're going to outthink them.'

He tossed the third scarab up in the air and caught it. Then he put his arm round Jo's shoulder and squeezed it as they looked at their motley resistance force.

'And I've got a really wild idea for what we do next . . .'